Dating Chase Walker

sex, love & timing

a novella by jillian conley

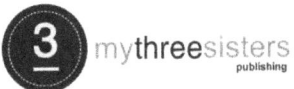

mythreesisters publishing

Printed in the United States of America.

www.jillianraeconley.com

Author photo by: Angela Rodriguez Keefe

ISBN-13: 978-0615807805
ISBN-10: 0615807801

Published by My Three Sisters Publishing

www.my3sisters.com

This novella is a work of fiction. Any references to people, organizations, establishments, or events are intended only to give this work of fiction a sense of authenticity and are used fictitiously. Names, characters, places, dialogue, and incidents portrayed are the product of the author's peculiar imagination and are not to be construed as real.

I should be hard at work on my latest romance novel, but every time I go to work on it I just end up staring at a blank page with a blinking cursor. My life has been so uninspired these past few months. It's like I am in a funk and I can't seem to pull myself out of it. I need to connect with love or lust to start feeling it in my mind and body so I can write about it, but I can't seem to find anything or anyone to connect with. Luckily, I have accomplished some sort of writing by finishing miscellaneous articles for my freelance job at the *RedEye* newspaper. Although, I have noticed the writing in my articles even seem jaded.

I can feel I am reaching the point of desperation and maybe that's why it seems to be getting worse. It is now mid-March and since New Year's, I have watched dozens of romantic comedies trying to connect with the characters, but none of them helped. I re-read my first two novels in an attempt to connect with the feelings I had when I wrote them, but I couldn't connect with my old self. I met my ex for dinner to see if I could feel any old feelings I had for him, but I felt nothing. I went to my uncle's beach house in California for a week of sun, the soothing sound of waves, and quiet, but everything I did write while there was crap and

I ended up deleting it.

In my more desperate attempt, I've become an Ok Cupid dating site whore. I've been on twenty-nine first dates in just over two months. Twenty-nine different men and I felt no excitement for or real attraction to any of them. I have become so jaded in my funk that they all just annoyed me for ridiculous reasons. There was Todd who had super small ears. Matthew chewed with his mouth open. Greg's nose hairs were hanging out of his nose. Andy laughed and a snot rocket flew out in the middle of dinner. Jon's breath smelled like grandpa breath. Mike spent our entire date talking about computer shit. And James laughed like he was jolly old Santa Claus. All the rest, I don't even know. I needed a fun night out to get my mind off my funk and my friend Bree's birthday party came at the perfect time.

My friend, Bree, is dating this guy Scotty Stylez who is the most eccentric man in Chicago nightlife. I don't know his real last name, but he goes by Stylez and it fits him perfectly. Scotty Stylez is a promoter and the only way I could describe him is POW! Everything he does or says is full of so much excitement. That's why I never just call him Scotty; I always call him Scotty Stylez. Bree's birthday is tonight and, of course, he has put together the "best party in town" for her. Since I stayed in all week attempting to start my new book and to pump out articles for the *RedEye,* but got pretty much nowhere, I was well rested and ready for a night out.

I put some booty shaking music on and got ready. I pulled out my shortest dress, highest pair of heels, and caked up my face. I was ready to party and release all the tension I had from writer's block with lots of vodka. Once I was ready I called Nikki who lived just a few blocks from me in our Wicker Park neighborhood. She got a cab and picked me up on the way. The girls were meeting at one of our favorite restaurants, Sunda, for dinner before heading to Moe's restaurant and bar for Bree's party. I loved how we would go to dinner before going out for the night, but we'd barely eat anything to prevent ourselves from busting out of our skimpy dresses.

When we got to Moe's, the place was packed. We grabbed some drinks and did what girls do best and congregated in a circle until a guy paid attention to us. Then, when a guy finally approached us, we'd pretend like we are lesbians to get them to leave us alone. It's really a fucked up little game women play. Drinks were free so I took two down in thirty minutes. I was feeling good. My good friend, Vodka, was suppressing all that stress.

As I was standing and talking to Nikki, a man approached me. He came up to me, put his right hand on my left hip and whispered in my ear, "I just wanted to tell you that you are beautiful." His touch sent butterflies through my entire body and his scent made me never want to exhale again. He slowly pulled his hand off my hip and away from me, but then placed his left arm on my upper right arm. He put his right hand out to shake mine as he said, "How are you? I'm Chase."

My entire body felt electrified and my panties were literally wet. I almost felt speechless, but I put my hand out to shake his and said, "I'm Audrey."

"Well, Audrey, I just wanted to tell you that you are beautiful. I hope to see you around," then he walked away with his little entourage.

My mind and body were in knots. What the fuck just happened? Who was that guy? I asked Nikki, "Do you know who that guy is?"

She rolled her eyes before responding, "Yeah, that's Chase Walker. He's a fucking creep and a huge playboy. Stay away from him."

"He's a hot creep. Why is he such a creep?"

"He's some dating and sex expert."

"What?"

"He's like Will Smith in the movie *Hitch*, but dirtier, much dirtier. Remember when Bree wanted us to go to that sex seminar? That was his seminar."

"Let me get this straight, he teaches people how to be better in bed? That's his job?"

"Yeah, something like that."

"That is ridiculously awesome. I have to interview this guy for the *RedEye*. He has a fucking entourage. How have I never heard of this guy?"

"I don't know. Stay away from him. He's probably a walking sexually transmitted infection."

The rest of the night, I was at attention trying to nonchalantly create another interaction with this Chase Walker guy. I was intrigued. I had to know more and I wanted him to touch me and send butterflies through my body again. There was no sign of him though; I even did a couple laps around the bar to try to spot him. I asked Scotty Stylez if he knew Chase and he enthusiastically said that Chase is legit. Scotty Stylez wasn't much help.

When I got home the first thing I did was hop on Google. I needed to find out more about this guy. My editor would love a story about him. I went through Chase Walker's entire website reading every single word, except the stuff I couldn't access without a membership. I was addicted to this guy's words. There was so much foul truth in it. His theories were pure genius. I wanted to access more, but I wasn't about to drop $200 on a membership.

I had been reading his articles and interviews for more than two hours, but I continued my stalking on Facebook and Twitter. Through my clicks on his Facebook page, I noticed he RSVP'd as attending a Charity 4 Life event on Tuesday. I had to go and I had to find a way to approach him without getting weak in my knees. My God, this guy was gorgeous. I felt my panties getting wet again. I hadn't had sex in months, let alone had any sort of attraction to a guy I had met. I was completely and utterly turned on just by thinking about him whispering in my ear and touching my hip. I wanted to douse my bed in his smell.

I decided to get naked and lay down in my bed. I closed my eyes, remembering his breath touching my skin as he whispered in my ear and the feeling of his hand touching my hip. I let it lead my imagination. My desire for him was so high that I could almost feel his lips touching mine before they slowly kissed their way down to my pussy. I put my hand down on my pussy and began to massage it. I pretended like it was his tongue moving around slowly. I inserted my index finger inside of my pussy imagining it was his finger moving it in and out slowly. Gradually, I moved faster and pushed my middle finger in with my index finger. The faster I moved, the more pleasure I could feel. My eyes were closed and I envisioned his face looking at me smiling while he bit his lip. I moved faster and used my other hand to rub the top of my clit. I felt so stimulated, I felt so alive and when I came I screamed out, "Chase!"

As I slowly came down from my orgasm high, I realized that I hadn't had a lone sexual experience like that in months. I had become so reliant on porn because I hadn't had someone who got me wet with one touch the way Chase Walker did. This guy's look, his touch, and words got to me like nothing ever before. I felt so alive and I wanted to feel more. I washed my hands and put on my pajamas. It was almost 5am. I curled up in my bed with a smile on my face and couldn't wait to see if he would let me interview him.

I got Bree to go to the Charity 4 Life event with me Tuesday night. Since she had been to Chase Walker's sex seminar, she was our common denominator and my best bet at helping me approach him. Bree thought I was nuts for stalking Chase down, but I kept telling her it was for an article. On the cab ride to The Grid, a posh underground restaurant and bar, I drilled Bree with questions about Chase's sex seminar that she attended. She had all great things to say about it. She shared a few of the things she had learned about how to perform on a man like the double fist with a twist and the treatment. Why didn't I attend the seminar with her? I must've figured when she invited me it was just something her boyfriend Scotty Stylez had her hyping up.

We walked into The Grid and I went directly to the bar. I needed to calm my nerves. I was feeling completely anxious trying to figure out how to approach Chase. *What if I got too nervous and forgot how to speak?* I ordered a shot. I needed to calm the fuck down and be professional. I wanted this interview badly. Bree and I mingled with some people all the while I had my eyes wandering around for Chase's appearance, but there was no sign of him. Two and a half hours had passed and Bree was getting antsy to go home because she had an early morning meeting. I begged her to stay with me just thirty more minutes until the event was over. She let out a huff, but agreed to stay if I agreed to go with her to an event that Friday at the new restaurant and bar, El Hefe. I had no plans that night anyway.

The charity event was coming to a close and there was still no sign of Chase. I was aggravated. I really wanted to talk to him in person and not have to call his representation requesting an interview. More than that, I wanted Chase to touch me and send butterflies through my body again. Bree and I put our coats on and headed out the door. The cab dropped her off at her apartment first and then dropped me off at my apartment. When I got home, I popped onto Chase's Facebook page to see if he was attending or hosting any upcoming events, but I couldn't find anything. I texted Bree and asked her to ask her boyfriend Scotty Stylez if he knew of any events of Chase's coming up. She responded, "Stop stalking Chase!"

I texted back, "Just ask your boyfriend."

"Fine!" A few minutes passed before Bree sent me a response after talking to her boyfriend. Her text said, "Scotty said that Chase will probably stop by the El Hefe event on Friday."

Friday night couldn't come soon enough. I was so excited about the possibility of seeing Chase that I was ready a half-hour before Bree and Natalie picked me up. I sat and ate a donut and drank a glass of wine anxiously waiting for them to arrive. In the cab, on the way to El Hefe, I reminded both Bree and Natalie to be on the lookout for Chase and to find me as soon as they saw him. They both thought I was nuts and Natalie had the same opinion of Chase as Nikki; that he was a playboy. I didn't care because this playboy's touch and words inspired me to feel more alive than I had felt in months. I felt so alive that I was able to write four chapters in my book during the week.

We were at El Hefe for two hours and there was no sign of Chase until Scotty Stylez came over and said, "Yo, Chase is here."

My stomach dropped to the floor. I walked over to the bathroom to release my nervous pee and make sure I looked okay. I stopped at the bar for a fresh drink before I went to find Chase. As I was ordering my drink, someone placed their hand on my forearm and I knew it was Chase by his scent and the butterflies that ran through my body. I turned to Chase and he smiled at me before saying, "Scotty Stylez told me that you are looking for me, Audrey?"

I felt choked up. I couldn't feel my body. I kept telling myself to breathe. I said to Chase, "Yes, one second." I turned to the bar to pay for my drink, but Chase gave the bartender one nod and the bartender shook his hand indicating that I didn't need to pay. We walked away from the bar, and I nervously attempted to form words in my mouth, but I was seriously having issues.

I think Chase took notice of my nervousness and said, "Wow, you are just so beautiful," then he sort of bit his lower lip. I could feel the cum seeping out of my pussy and onto my panties.

I said, "Thank you."

Chase said, "So you've been looking for me?"

"Yes, we briefly met last weekend."

"I remember."

"Well, after our meeting, I heard a little bit about what you do. I write for the *RedEye,* and I'd love to interview you for a story."

Chase squinted his eyes a little as he said, "Hmmm."

I said, "Well, I've read everything on your site except the membership stuff and I am going to do an article on you whether or not you do the interview. I can get across more of what you want the readers to hear about you if you let me interview you. It can be quick, even over the phone."

Chase put his finger up to his chin like he was thinking for a second before he said, "I'll agree to have a drink with you."

I could work with that. I said, "Okay, a drink."

"Alright, Audrey, let's do this."

I asked, "Right now?"

Chase laughed as he said, "No, not right now." He then waved for a girl to come over. When the girl was near us he continued, "Audrey, this is my assistant Mary. She'll set us up to meet for a drink next week."

Chase lightly grabbed my forearm, pulled me in close, and gave me a gentle kiss on the cheek before walking away. I needed to go wipe out the cum on my panties. I gave Mary my information and she said she would give me a call Monday morning. I was no longer freaked out about getting the interview, but I was now freaked out about the interview itself. How did

Chase Walker's presence have such an effect on me?

Chase's assistant, Mary, called me Monday morning and told me Chase would be at the swanky hotel bar, Sable, at 4pm on Wednesday for our meeting. I read through his website a few more times before Wednesday and went fully prepared with a list of questions. I arrived a half-hour early to have a drink and settle in. As I was sitting on a couch in the corner for privacy, I watched the door for Chase. He arrived right at 4 o'clock and it was just him: no assistant and no entourage. I was happy because I wanted to get the scoop on this guy all alone. When Chase spotted me he smiled and walked toward me. On his way toward me he gave a wave to the bartender. I stood up to welcome him. He grabbed my hip, kissed my cheek lightly, and then said, "How are you?"

I responded, "I'm good."

Chase stood waiting for me to take my seat first like a gentleman. I was impressed. When he sat down he sat rather close to me. I leaned down to grab my iPad with my list of questions and Chase stopped me and said, "No iPad. This isn't an interview. We are having a drink together."

I asked, "Can I at least record our conversation?"

Chase lightly shook his head no before smiling at me and saying, "Relax. My God, you are beautiful."

I felt my face turn bright red before saying, "Okay, I will relax." I took a deep breath and smiled at him. I didn't know what else to do. The bartender walked over with a drink for Chase and when he left I asked, "Do you just walk around the city nodding and waving and people just do what you want?"

"He's just one of my guys."

"He's a client?"

"Yes, he was, but he's married now."

"How long have you been a dating and sex expert?"

"I'll answer this question, but no more of your prepared questions. I started in the fitness industry about ten years ago. I was a fitness and lifestyle coach. My business ended up going belly up and I transitioned from fitness and lifestyle to lifestyle and sex."

I don't know why I decided to say this, but it came out of my mouth, "Your mannerisms and scent literally make my panties wet."

He smiled and said, "Now that is one of the best compliments I have ever received."

I asked, "Do women just throw themselves at you all the time?"

Chase looked to the right briefly before saying, "I love women, all women, and all I want to do is appreciate them in every way possible."

"Yeah, but you are a hot sex expert with swag. I bet they throw themselves at you all the time."

"I am going to kiss you right now." I felt my eyes widen and, before I knew it, his lips we gently touching mine. They felt even better than I imagined. He kissed so soft, so gentle. I felt the butterflies rush through my body. I wanted to stay locked into the kiss for the rest of my life. When he pulled away from our kiss, I had to remind myself to breathe. As I took a breath he said, "Your lips are as soft as I imagined."

I wasn't sure what was going on here. I came into this thinking I was interviewing this guy and he just kissed me. No complaints, only confusion. Chase smiled at me as he took a sip of his drink then said, "I am very drawn to you."

I asked, "Do you say that to all the girls?"

"No, not all the girls. There's something about you that draws me to you. That's why I stopped to talk to you at Moe's that night just so I could tell you that you are beautiful."

"You say all the right things in the right way. If you asked, I'd probably go have sex with you in the bathroom right now."

Chase let out a boyish chuckle that was endearing before he said, "I wouldn't have sex with you right now."

I said, "That's kind of offensive."

"Not in the least bit. If I were lucky enough to have you, I'd want to take my time and appreciate every last inch of your beautiful body."

"So you aren't into quickies?"

"Don't get me wrong, I love a good quickie, but I am into the right timing for sex. I'd want to seduce you and get to know your body before I fucked you for the first time. A lot of people think that I am some playboy that sleeps with multiple women because I seduce them. That's actually what most people like to see, but personally, right now in my life I don't want to conquer many women because that's too easy. I want to conquer one woman; mind, body and spirit."

"So are you looking for a long-term relationship?"

"I'm always looking for the right girl to spend time with."

His answers increased my desire for him. I wanted to be the woman he conquered. I hadn't been seduced or fucked in months, let alone fucked right in years. I had such a strong desire for this man and I barely knew him. His touch, his mannerisms, and his words all drew me in so deep. After so many months, I was finally feeling again and I didn't want it to stop. I wanted to feel more and more. I leaned down to grab my drink and I noticed my hand was shaking. Chase grabbed my hand with his and brought it up to his mouth to kiss it before saying, "I think it's cute that you are nervous. I'll admit I am a little nervous around you, too."

He didn't look nervous at all so I asked with a bit of confusion, "You are nervous around me?"

"You are a beautiful woman and I am intrigued by you. I may not show nerves physically, but I feel it in my gut."

"Knowing that actually makes me feel a little more comfortable."

"Good, get comfortable with me. I want to get to know you."

"I'm the one who wants to get to know you so I can write an article on you."

"Why are you so hung up on doing an article on me? There are so many articles about me out there. Do me a favor and stop thinking about the article. Just spend time with me and later if you decide you still want to write the article, then that's fine. But I think you and I getting to know each other for us would be better than walking away with just an article."

"Okay, it's just I've spent the last few months completely uninspired in life and with my writing. After you whispered in my ear that night, I got a surge of energy in me. Reading your website and finding out more about you has made me feel so good inside. You inspire me and I feel like I could actually write something really good if I write about you."

"That makes me feel good knowing I inspire you and I know you could write a great article on me, but hold off for a little bit. I promise I won't give any interviews to anyone else at the *RedEye*."

"Okay, but why hold off?"

Chase grabbed both my hands and said, "Just trust me. I need to head out, but meet me in front of the Trump Tower at noon on Sunday for an afternoon date." He then leaned in and kissed me on the cheek before standing up. Chase walked toward the door, turning back at me with a smile before exiting.

I was disappointed in his sudden departure. I hoped we'd be there for hours with me picking his brain. I guess I had enough to ponder on until Sunday. I realized that he never asked if he could kiss me and never asked me for a date, he simply suggested it and went ahead. How sly. And the fact that he said he wouldn't have sex with me right now boggled my mind. Most men would be all over no-strings-attached sex in an instant. My God, this man turned me on.

When I got home, I undressed noticing that my panties were creamy, but dry. I lay down on my bed fully naked and imagined what Chase would feel like exploring my body. How he would conquer me. If his kiss was any indication, it would be slow, soft and powerful. I imagined Chase on top of me. How he would look naked. The curves of his muscles and what his cock would look like; how it would feel inside of me. Would he move slowly inside of me? Would he go deep? As I imagined all this, I began to rub my clit. Over and over I imagined his body and his cock moving in and out of my pussy making me more and more wet with each thrust. I grabbed my dildo out of the nightstand and slowly inserted it into my pussy. I felt my cum cover it as it welcomed the dildo in. I pretended it was Chase's cock slowly moving deep inside of me. Gradually, I made the dildo move faster and deeper inside of me as I kept visioning his body on top of mine. I let out a loud moan and soon I felt my body tense up and then my pussy pulsate with orgasm.

I lay taking in my orgasm high for a few minutes. Just the thought of Chase had given me two amazing orgasms recently. I wanted more. I needed more. I was feeling alive again and it was with the help of just his presence. I couldn't wait for our date Sunday and hoped he'd explore and conquer my body that afternoon.

It felt like it took forever for Sunday to arrive, but I kept busy by writing. I finally made some progress on my novel. I had written two more chapters and I was beginning to feel a creative flow. Chase was exactly what I needed to start moving out of my creativity funk. I couldn't wait to see him again in hopes that his presence would inspire even more in me.

I got up early Sunday morning and took a long shower. I shaved every inch of my body preparing for the possibility that he would explore my physical body and pleasure me in many ways. If a small touch from him on my hip sent so much energy through my body, I could only imagine the pure ecstasy he could create in me through a sexual experience. I wanted him to touch my pussy, whether it be with his fingers, tongue, or cock. I was ready for him to take control of my body.

I took twenty minutes deciding what to wear because I wasn't sure what we would be doing. I assumed we'd be having lunch at the Trump since we were meeting there. I decided on something a little more casual since it was the afternoon. I arrived a couple minutes after noon and Chase was waiting outside for me. The doorman came over and opened the door to let me out of the cab. When I got out, Chase smiled at me as he walked toward me. I smiled back. He walked up close up to me, put his hand on my neck and pulled me in for a sweet, soft kiss. After he kissed me he smiled again and said, "You are just so beautiful."

I felt my face turn red and I smiled back at him. I could feel the butterflies moving through my body. Chase gently grabbed my hand and led me as we walked away from the Trump building. I asked, "Where are we going?"

Chase responded, "The grocery store."

I said with confusion, "What?"

"I am going to make you lunch, but we need to go to the grocery store together so I can find out more about what you like. The grocery store is the perfect place for a first date ... or in our case, a second date."

I liked that Chase considered our first lone meeting a first date. I asked, "Why did we meet at the Trump?"

"I live there." *I thought shit, this guy must have money. The Trump had the most luxurious condos in Chicago.*

We walked hand in hand down the street to the grocery store. When we walked inside the store, Chase grabbed a cart and we began walking down the first aisle. We started in the liquor section and he asked, "What kind of wine do you prefer?"

"I usually get Pinot Grigio as a white and Cabernet as red."

Chase grabbed a bottle of each and we continued on. He asked, "What are you in the mood to eat for lunch today?"

"Donuts."

Chase asked, "Donuts for lunch?"

I said, "Yeah, donuts."

Chase laughed as if he thought I was joking before continuing, "I can cook anything. Are you a vegetarian?"

"My parents are hippies so I only got to eat meat once a week growing up. Once I moved out on my own, I kind of became a meat hoarder. I think sometimes I feel like I was deprived of it as a child and that's why I eat it so much now."

"Do you want chicken, beef or fish?"

"Since it's day-time, chicken seems lighter, let's do that."

"I'm glad you didn't say fish. I'm not a fish eater."

"Why would you give it as an option then?"

"Because getting and making this meal is about me getting to know and explore you and your tastes." He looked to be in thought for a second, then asked, "How about vegetables?"

"I like all vegetables except cabbage. It makes me gassy."

Chase let out a little laugh and said, "Noted, no cabbage."

"And fruits?"

"I am a big fruit fan. I eat a lot of fruit, but mostly apples, pineapple, and grapes."

"Alright, I know what I am going to make you."

We made our way to the back of the store. When we walked past an end-of-the-aisle display of cereal, Chase asked me about my favorite cereals as a kid. We both were Lucky Charms fans. I told him how I could cook, but only a few things. He went on to tell me that he was an amazing cook and felt that cooking together was a very sensual experience for couples. He actually had many of his clients take cooking classes so they could be more sensual with their partners in the kitchen. I had cooked with guys I dated in the past, but never really looked at it as a sensual experience because I always ended up burning things and getting yelled at.

Chase picked up some chicken, a pineapple, some nuts and other miscellaneous items as we walked. We checked out and headed back to his place. I couldn't wait to see his condo. I was curious to see how he lived. He seemed so in control of himself so it made me wonder if his environment was the same. When we walked into his condo, it was enormous! Everything looked brand new and there were boxes scattered around. He apologized for the mess, saying he just moved in a few weeks ago. I asked, "Where did you live before?"

"Before I moved into The Trump, I lived outside of the city in a small apartment with a friend of mine. If you had met me a few months ago, you might think of me differently."

"What do you mean?"

"Well, before my new site and program launched in January I only had a handful of clients I coached; I was focusing on building the Chase Walker membership program and website. Every cent I made went into my company. I've been working on it for three years and until the big launch in January, I was kind of broke and not many people knew of me."

"So everything just took off for you

recently?"

"Yep, New Year's Day my company's new website launched and almost every single day after that in January I had a different newspaper interview, radio interview, blog interview, or TV interview. I was crazy busy, but we sold over 2,000 memberships in the first month."

"Shit, that's like $400,000!"

"Yeah, and we sold almost 3,000 memberships in February."

"Wow, I am amazed that I never heard of you before you whispered in my ear that night at Moe's."

"I like knowing I had that affect on you and you didn't know who I was."

"I went home that night and Googled you. I was on your site for over two hours addicted to your words."

"I love hearing that."

Chase opened the bottle of Pinot Grigio that he bought at the grocery store and poured me a glass. He offered to give me a tour before we started cooking. His place was pretty big and when I walked into his bedroom, it felt like I walked into a cloud of his scent. My pussy jumped a little. I think it jumped from the scent and seeing where he sleeps. I wanted to kiss him and throw him down on the bed at that very moment. I was horny so I got ballsy and I grabbed his hand, pulled him closer to me and kissed him. He kissed me back passionately and then smiled like he knew what I was trying to do, but led me back into the kitchen. What was with this guy? I was practically throwing myself at him and he wasn't budging.

We cooked lunch together and it actually was very sensual. We tasted the food along the way and there was a lot of touching of one another. He hit my boob with his hand and I thought it was accidental because he didn't look like he even noticed he was doing it. When it happened another two times I started to wonder if it was actually accidental. With each touch from him, I felt a rush go through my body. My God, I couldn't wait to feel this guy inside of me. If a quick brush of the hand could send such a rush through my body, I couldn't imagine what him being inside of me would feel like.

After lunch, we sat down on his couch to rest. I rested my head on his leg and he ran his fingers through my hair. I loved the way he looked at me. He made me feel so beautiful when he looked at me. We were silent and I was enjoying it, but I wanted to know more about him. I asked, "What's your story?"

"What do you mean 'my story?'"

"I know you moved from fitness and lifestyle coach to lifestyle and sex coach, but how did you get there?"

"I'll tell you my full story once I know you won't be doing an article on me."

"So it's juicy stuff?"

"Not at all. It's just personal and stuff I don't think should be published about me during the introduction stage of my company."

Chase moved his hand down from rubbing my head to my stomach. He slowly lifted my shirt up, but stopped right below my breasts. He ran his fingers up and down my bare belly. It felt so good and I could feel the butterflies moving through my body and a little bit of cum drip out of my pussy. I hoped this was the start to us fucking. I was so ready. Every time his fingers moved toward my lower abdomen I wished they'd go into my pants. He stayed on my belly, though. I put my hand on his and tried directing him lower, but he just looked down, smiled at me and shook his head no. I looked back, bit my lower lip and said, "Please."

He asked, "What's your rush, Audrey?"

"It's been a long time since I've had sex or even foreplay and you are just so sexy. I really want to know how you would feel inside of me." This guy had some will power. I've been throwing myself at him and he keeps telling me to be patient. I started to wonder if he was attracted to me.

Chase smiled as he said, "Patience."

I asked, "Are you not attracted to me?"

"Sit up for a second and give me your hand." He took my hand and placed it over his pants. I could feel his cock. It was hard and it felt big, really big.

"See, you want it, too. Let's just get naked!"

"Lay your head back down on my lap and close your eyes." I did as instructed. "I would want nothing more than to take each piece of your clothing off slowly while I kiss your soft lips. Once I had you naked, I would kiss every inch of your body starting with your neck. Slowly working my way down your chest, I'd stop to appreciate your perfect breasts licking your nipples until they became hard." My pussy was now dripping. Chase continued speaking slowly in a sensual voice ... "As I moved down the curves on your stomach, I'd run my hands up and down your thighs, watching as little goose bumps appear all over your body. I'd continue down, giving your pussy a quick kiss as I pass it by and move down your right leg. Once I got down to your right foot, I'd massage it, gently, as I spread your legs open and admire your beautiful pussy. I'd continue to admire it while I massage your left foot. I'd then work my way up your left leg and put my lips back on your pussy. I'd use my tongue and lips to pleasure you until you came. That will be our first sexual experience."

I took a deep breath before saying, "Holy shit, my pussy is literally dripping. I think I need to go to the bathroom."

Chase smiled at me as I walked to the bathroom. When I got in there, I locked the door and quickly masturbated. I couldn't take it. I had to get off. I was so turned on by his touch and description of our first sexual experience that it only took me about twenty seconds of masturbation before I came. I took a piece of tissue and wiped the cum out of my panties and off my pussy, washed my hands, and headed back out to the living room. Chase looked at me as I walked in the room and just smiled at me, making me feel like he had never seen something so beautiful.

We talked for a little while longer before I left. He said he would drive me home, but he hadn't had a chance to buy a new car yet. He walked me downstairs and kissed me before I got into a cab. I wanted to text him on the ride home, but realized I didn't have his number. He had mine, but I never got his. A few minutes later, I got a text from a number and knew it was him. It said, "I had a great time with you today, Audrey. See you soon."

I wondered how far away soon was, but I played it cool and simply wrote, "I did too. Thank you for lunch."

On Monday morning, I woke-up to a text saying, "Good morning, beautiful. I hope you have a lovely day." I got the same thing on Tuesday and Wednesday morning.

I always responded with a, "You too."

It wasn't until Wednesday night that Chase sent me a text that said, "I'd like to see you tomorrow night. Meet me at my place at 8pm."

I responded, "I'll be there."

I started getting excited that I'd finally get to see him again. On Thursday morning, I took a break from writing to browse Facebook. In the right corner of my home page it said that today was Chase's birthday. I was surprised he didn't tell me, but excited that he wanted to spend it with me. I wondered what we'd be doing. Maybe I would be his date to a big birthday party for him? I started to worry about what I should wear. I decided to text Chase and ask how I should dress for the night. He said we would be going out. I thought to myself, fun! I got to go out with *THE* Chase Walker and be like a celebrity for a night!

I got myself all dolled up and decided to wear some sexy lingerie under my dress. Knowing it was his birthday, I felt the odds were higher that he might actually let us get past all this talk and we'd fuck. I was supposed to get my period over the weekend, so I wanted to have sex before my vagina was out of commission for a few days.

Before leaving for Chase's, I ran across the street to grab an Oreo ice cream birthday cake from Baskin Robbins to surprise him for his birthday. I thought it would be a nice gesture. Since it was a combo Baskin Robbins and Dunkin Donuts I bought a long john to eat on the cab ride over. When I arrived at the Trump building, I had to sign in at the front desk. They called up and Chase gave the okay to let me through. When I got to his floor he was waiting by the elevator for me. I smiled when I saw him and he smiled back. He asked, "What's in the box?"

I replied, "Happy Birthday!"

"How did you know it's my birthday?"

"I saw it on Facebook."

"Oh, that Facebook."

When we got into his condo, he opened the box. I said, "It's an Oreo ice cream cake."

He asked, "How did you know that's my favorite?"

"Lucky guess."

"We'll eat it when we get back tonight."

I gave him a sly look and said, "When *WE* get back tonight?"

"Yes, you are coming home with me tonight."

"I was just checking to make sure I heard you right."

We headed out of Chase's condo and walked over to Vertigo Sky Lounge, one of Chicago's most posh lounges that is located on the top floor of the Dana Hotel. When we arrived, his friend greeted him and showed us to a quaint table in the corner. Our table was the best in the house and it gave us an incredible view of the skyline with the floor to ceiling windows. We sat down and a server brought us a bottle of Grey Goose® vodka. I asked, "How many people are coming out tonight?"

Chase responded, "It's just us."

With confusion I asked, "A whole bottle of Grey Goose® for just us?"

"We don't have to drink it all. My friend insisted on giving it to me for my birthday. I just want an intimate night with you for my birthday. I am not big on birthdays and I will be out with plenty of people this weekend. Let's just have a couple drinks and enjoy each other's company."

We drank our first round of drinks and I felt a little relaxed, but every time he touched me, even just the littlest bit, I still felt butterflies. I couldn't wait to get back to his place. By drink three, we probably should've stopped drinking for the night. We were both getting pretty tipsy, but I liked that he was loosening up and talking a big game about how good he was in bed. It was turning me on. He had been so patient and proper during our last interactions, but after a few drinks, I got to see the dirty side of him. He kept touching and kissing me at the table. When I felt his hand move up my skirt to massage my pussy through my panties I knew it was time for us to go. I wanted him to put this big game he was talking on me. We finished our drinks, took a shot, and headed out the door.

After leaving Vertigo, I only remember bits and pieces of the rest of the night. I remember we stopped for a make-out session on the walk back to his place. I remember getting into his place and him taking my clothes off. I know he went down on me, but I don't remember if it was good, bad or indifferent. I know I sucked his cock, but I couldn't get it hard so I told him to just fuck me and he did. His cock didn't stay hard for long, though. We both fell asleep, but I woke up in the middle of the night with cramps and I couldn't fall back asleep. I was worried I was about to get my period and I was really embarrassed about our sex so I slipped my clothes on and snuck out the door to go home.

When I got into the cab, I looked at my hand and it had dry blood all over it. I looked down in between my legs and there was blood all over the insides of my thighs. OH MY FUCKING GOD I GOT MY PERIOD! I started to worry that I had gotten my period on his bed. How did we not notice? If there was this much on me, I couldn't imagine what his cock looked like. I was freaking out. I probably would never hear from him again. Shit! Shit! Shit! Shit!

I showered as soon as I got home, but when I lay on my bed, I couldn't fall asleep. I kept worrying that I left blood on Chase's bed, his cock; oh shit, he went down on me! There could be blood on his mouth! How could my vagina do this to me? Was my vagina mad at him for holding out on her last Sunday and she was getting back at him? Why, Vagina? Why? I lay on my bed so embarrassed and pissed off until I literally could not keep my eyes open.

I woke up to my phone ringing a few hours later. It was Chase. I was scared to answer, but I pressed the answer button and timidly said, "Hello."

He replied, "Good morning, beautiful."

Oh my God, maybe there was no blood! He sounded like everything was normal. I said, "Good morning."

He asked, "Why did you sneak out last night?"

I hesitated as I said, "Umm, err ... I couldn't sleep."

"I was worried you might be dead."

"No, why would I be dead?"

"Well, umm there was blood all over me and my bed so I was convinced I killed you in my sleep and hid your body somewhere." He let out a laugh indicating he was joking.

My heart dropped. Oh the embarrassment! "I am so sorry!"

"Don't be. I am just kidding with you. It's all good. I would like to request a mulligan though."

I had no idea what a mulligan was so I asked, "What's that?"

"A do-over of last night, once your period is over, of course."

"Really?"

"I don't remember much of last night, but I am sure my performance was not well. Let's just erase last night from our memories and we will have a redo of our first time."

"Thank you for being so nice, Chase. I am so embarrassed right now."

"Don't be embarrassed and just erase it from your mind. Remember, it never happened."

"Okay."

"Well, I need to get some work done. You

go take care of yourself and we will talk later."

"Have a good day, Chase."

"You too, Audrey."

I felt relieved after I hung up the phone. Chase was so nice about everything, but I still couldn't believe what had happened. The first time you sleep with someone it is usually awkward, but this was a fucking disaster. I snuggled back into my bed and fell asleep until 2 p.m. when I woke up with excruciating cramps. I took some Ibuprofen, put a heating pad on my abdomen, and turned on the movie *Breakfast at Tiffany's*. Oh the joys of being a woman.

I didn't hear from Chase the rest of the weekend and I was kind of worried. He seemed so nice about what happened, but maybe he had changed his mind. I kept my mind off him the best I could by pounding out three more chapters in my book. I was finally on a roll. On Monday morning, my editor at the *RedEye* had sent me some stories to do so I worked on those throughout the day. Finally, in the afternoon, I got a text from Chase that said, "Hello, beautiful. How's that period?"

I wanted to ask where he disappeared to all weekend, but I simply replied, "Better."

He asked, "Would you like me to come over and snuggle with you tonight?"

Aww! Chase offering to come over and cuddle made me feel better about him not contacting me all weekend. I said, "I'd love that."

"I'll bring pizza. I should be there around 8."

"See you then."

I scrambled around my apartment cleaning up and washing my bedding. I was in bed a lot over the weekend, so I am sure it was covered in my sleep smell. Chase showed up right on time and when he walked in he said, "You look so amazing even in your pajamas," and then he kissed me softly.

I just loved when Chase was around. My body felt so alive. We went into the kitchen and opened the bottle of wine he brought, Cabernet, he remembered my favorite red wine. We sat down at the table and I opened the box of pizza. I said, "That's odd. The pizza is cut in pie shape. Usually they cut it in squares."

Chase responded, "I don't eat square-cut pizza."

I was puzzled by his remark so I asked, "You don't eat square-cut pizza? Is it different or something?"

"It is absolutely different. Eating pizza should be an experience. You should be able to hold the piece by the crust and eat your way through it. Being able to hold the crust keeps you from getting greasy fingers, too."

"Square-cut pizzas have crusts too."

"Not all the pieces. What about all those crustless pieces in the middle that nobody wants?"

Meeting a square-cut pizza hater was a first for me. I asked, "Have you always hated square-cut pizza?"

"Yes, as a kid, I'd always get screwed and get stuck with the crappy middle pieces. When it is pie-cut, everyone gets an even amount of pizza and nobody gets stuck with the crustless middle."

I thought his hate for square-cut pizza was odd, but his theory made sense. I simply said, "I've never thought about it that way."

We ate the pie-cut pizza while he told me about his day. I so badly wanted to ask about his weekend or why he didn't call or text me for a few days, but I didn't want to sound like a crazy girl. Instead, I was just happy he was here now. After we ate, we went and cuddled in my bed. We lay face-to-face and Chase asked me, "What made you want to write romance novels?"

I said, "Well, I am a sap for a good love story and I think sex is so important in a relationship. I push the limits with each book I write and hopefully I will feel comfortable enough doing full-on erotica in the future. I just haven't had the opportunity to explore it personally enough yet. All in all, words just turn me on. That Sunday, when you described what you would be doing to me during our first sexual experience, well, when I went into the bathroom, I masturbated."

Chase smiled as he said, "I know."

I blushed as I asked, "You know I masturbated?" *I thought I had been so sly about it.*

"I saw your glowing face when you came out. I find it hot that you are so open sexually."

"I love sex, but I feel like I am too sexual sometimes."

"Never, ever say that. You can never be too sexual."

"Well, I'd always want to try new things in the past and the guys I was with would be fun at first, but then slowly turned into men who fucked and fell asleep. I think that's why I could never keep a guy around for more than a few months."

"That saddens me to hear that. Sex is meant to be variable, it's meant to be explored, and the limits should constantly be pushed. If you were mine, I'd explore anything you wanted to at anytime on any day."

I smiled as I said, "I tried to bring the hand job back last year ..."

With excitement Chase responded, "I always say we need to bring the hand job back!"

"Well, I tried, but the guys I tried it with didn't seem like fans. I must've been doing it wrong."

"You can practice on me if you'd like. I can give you pointers if you need them."

I hoped it was a sexual invitation, but to confirm I asked, "Right now?"

"Sure."

I leaned in and we started kissing. It was soft at first and slowly became more passionate. I moved my hand down to rub his cock over his pants. It got hard fast. While we were kissing he pulled my shirt off over my head. As he looked at my naked chest he said, "Your tits are just perfect."

I unbuttoned his pants and he helped me to pull them down. I lightly stroked his cock as I felt it getting harder and bigger in my hand. I leaned down and put my mouth on it for a minute to get it wet with my spit. Once it was wet, I moved back up and continued kissing his lips. I stroked his cock lightly, gradually tightened my grip. I pulled away from kissing him and whispered in his ear, "Your cock is so big, so hard, so perfect," and I felt it increase in size. I put my other hand on his cock to give it a double fisted stroke and he let out a moan that let me know I was doing a good job. I kept stroking him slowly and loved watching his face as he lay back and relaxed. I was getting turned on just watching him. I stroked further down and rubbed his balls, he moaned again. I so badly wanted to put my mouth on his cock, but I wanted to show him that I could give a good hand job. I increased my speed, tightened my grip, and twisted as I moved up and down his cock. I went faster and faster and his moans got closer together. I kept at it as hard as I could until I heard him say, "I'm going to cum."

I put my mouth over the head of his cock and let him cum in my mouth. I swallowed his cum and, when he opened his eyes, he smiled at me and said, "You definitely weren't doing it wrong."

I laughed and curled up into his arms. It felt so good being held by him, I felt alive and I felt safe. I think if I had to stay in one spot for the rest of my life, it would be cuddled in his arms. He made for a great big spoon. We lay there for a little while and he rubbed my arm gently. I told him about my family and he told me about his family. It felt good being held physically, but it also felt good to be connecting with someone. It had been so long since I really connected with anyone. I must've felt safe and comfortable because I fell asleep mid-conversation.

I woke up in the morning to the alarm blaring on Chase's phone. He was still holding me tight and not budging to get up to turn off his alarm. I lightly elbowed him, but I got no response. He was a heavy sleeper. I attempted to turn over, but it was hard getting out of the lock he had me in inside of his arms. Finally, he budged and I said, "Your alarm is going off."

He mumbled back, "Five more minutes."

With agitation I said, "I can't reach your

phone to turn your alarm off."

He said again, "Five more minutes."

"Dude, I can't get to it to turn it off."

"What, oh, okay." Chase reached behind him and turned the alarm off so I was able to break out of his arms to turn around to look at him. His eyes were halfway open when I turned over. He puckered up his lips and said, "Kiss me, you beautiful girl."

I kissed him and then snuggled into his chest. I took in his smell and hoped my bed would smell like him after he left. I asked, "What time do you have to work today?"

He stretched his arms above his head before saying, "I'm filming at ten."

"Filming what?"

"A pilot for a reality show."

"You are going to have your own reality show?"

"Possibly. We are just filming the pilot to pitch to networks."

"That's so cool."

"Yeah, don't get me wrong, I love the attention, but I am still getting used to it. I really enjoy the quiet time I've been spending with you. I can just be me around you."

"I'm glad you feel that way. I still get butterflies around you, but I'm surprised how comfortable I've gotten with you. I was so nervous during our first few interactions."

Chase said, "That's cute, but get used to having me around."

I I woke-up on Thursday to a text from Chase asking if my period was gone. I still had some spotting the day before so I went to the bathroom to check it out before I responded. It looked like I was in the clear. He told me to come over that night to have the mulligan. I got excited thinking that tonight would be the night I'd finally get to fully experience the hype of Chase Walker. I utilized my enthusiasm by spending the day writing and I finally made it to the climax of my story. I called my agent to let her know I was making headway and she requested that I send her what I had so far. I showered and got ready then spent another half-hour writing before I headed out the door to Chase's.

I signed in at the front desk when I got into his building and took the elevator up. Chase was waiting for me by the elevator door when I got to his floor. He smiled at me when the doors opened and I ran out, jumped on him, and kissed him with excitement. He said, "Someone is ready to get laid."

I replied, "You have no idea."

"I have it all planned out, baby. Just relax and enjoy the ride."

We walked down the hall to his condo and, when he opened the door, there were candles everywhere. It was so romantic. He took my coat off and handed me a glass of wine. After he hung up my coat, he grabbed my hand and led me into his bedroom. I felt butterflies flutter through my entire body and my panties were getting wet just thinking about him conquering me. Chase had some lingerie laid out on his bed. He told me to put the lingerie on and then to come and join him in the living room. I did as he requested and I was surprised that he knew my exact size. I felt so sexy in this new lingerie.

I took a big sip of my wine before walking out to join Chase in the living room. It helped me to relax, but I wasn't about to drink too much. I wanted to feel and remember every single second of this experience. He had talked himself up quite a bit and I wanted to take it all in. When I walked into the living room he stood up and looked at me with a smile as he said, "Shit, your body is so perfect. Have I told you yet today that you are beautiful? 'Cause you are. My God, you are fucking beautiful!"

I loved when he told me I was beautiful. It sent a charge through my body and made me feel more confident each time he said it. He grabbed my hand and brought me over to sit on the couch. I anxiously awaited his touch, but then he asked me, "How was your day?"

What? My day? Who cares about my day? Just start touching me! I answered him though saying, "It was good. I reached the climax of my book today, and my agent was very happy about it."

"Great. And how are you feeling?"

"Horny, now let's get to this."

"Slow down, baby. I promise you won't leave here until you are completely satisfied.

Just trust me."

I sort of huffed as I said, "Okay, I trust you. How was your day?"

"Busy, but it sounds like there is some interest in the pilot we've been filming. Oh, and I am going to be on a radio show tomorrow morning so if you don't leave in the middle of the night, make sure I get up when my alarm goes off. Last time I was on this show I was late. I am not a morning person."

"I don't know how you could sleep through that alarm of yours."

"I can sleep through almost anything. My old roommate was a DJ and he played music all hours of the night."

"I'll make sure you are up. I'm a light sleeper."

"Okay, finish your wine. I'm getting anxious to taste your pussy now."

I chugged the rest of my wine and smiled at Chase. He directed me to lie on the blanket he had laid on the floor and then he put a pillow under my head. He told me to close my eyes and take deep breaths. I did as told and while I was breathing he put his lips on mine and kissed me softly. I loved his kisses. Then I felt his lips move away from mine and shortly after, I felt him down by my feet. He complimented my feet and then began to massage them. I felt my body relaxing by the minute.

After a good twenty minutes or more of massaging my feet, I felt his lips touch mine again. We kissed slowly and softly and I felt his hands lightly touching my chest. He pulled his lips away from mine and moved his kisses down my neck. I felt butterflies and shivers run through my body. Away from my neck, he moved down toward my breasts stopping at one of my nipples to lick and suck on it. I felt my nipples grow harder with each movement of his tongue. While they were wet, he gently blew on them making them reach their hardest point. I could feel the cum exiting my pussy.

Continuing on, he kissed every last inch of my stomach, hitting one spot that triggered me to moan. His hands were caressing my hips and making their way down to my thighs. His mouth stopped for a quick kiss on my pussy where he said, "I'm going to wreck you tonight," before moving to kiss my inner thighs. I felt him spreading my legs apart and then covering every last inch of my inner thighs with his tongue. He kept on moving down where he kissed and rubbed my feet some more. I was dying to feel him inside of me. He worked his way back up to my pussy where he lightly moved his tongue around my labia. He said, "You taste so amazing."

When I felt his tongue on my clit I shivered with pleasure. He was gentle with it at first, but then began to suck on it, causing several moans to exit my mouth. He knew exactly how to handle a clit. His tongue went up and down my labia and clit for several minutes. I opened my eyes and looked down at him and smiled. He looked back up at me with a smile and a look like he was in heaven. With each movement of his tongue, I could feel the cum slowly dripping out of my pussy.

He kept at it with enthusiasm like he never wanted to stop and I never wanted him to stop. Adding his thumb into the mix with his tongue sent pleasure through my whole body. I began moaning loudly and once he picked up speed I realized I could no longer hold in my orgasm. It felt so good and I didn't have the strength to hold back. My body tensed up with pleasure and I released a bittersweet orgasm. I lay relaxed, enjoying coming down from the high of my orgasm. As I lay there, I felt Chase gently blow on my pussy causing it to pulsate. As he blew softly on my pussy, he lightly brushed his fingers up and down my thighs before pressing a warm washcloth on my pussy. My body was in pure ecstasy. His actions exceeded his descriptive words and now I wanted to thank him for it.

I sat up and kissed his mouth, tasting myself on his lips. We kissed passionately as I moved my hands down to his already hard cock. I loved the way his cock felt in my palm, the way it grew larger and harder with my touch. I stroked it gently up and down for a few moments and then asked him to stand up. Once he was standing I put my mouth on his cock. I sucked slowly for several minutes as I felt the head of his cock grow larger. I looked up at him and he smiled at me, I smiled back. I was so turned on seeing that I created so much pleasure in him. I used more suction with my mouth and added my right hand so I could satisfy his entire cock. I gradually increased my speed and twisted my hand as I stroked his cock up and down. He moaned with pleasure, and when his moans became more frequent, I increased my speed until I felt an explosion of his cum and pulsating of his cock in my mouth. I loved feeling him cum inside my mouth.

We lay down on the blanket for a few minutes and he held me tight as he came down from his orgasm high. We were both feeling amazing. I rubbed his arm up and down as we laid there in silence for several minutes before he said, "I'm not done with you yet."

I turned over and smiled at him. He kissed me and then moved to get up. He put out his hand to help me up. He told me to go refill our wine glasses and then meet him in the bathroom. I did as he requested. When I walked into the bathroom, the water was running in his gigantic Jacuzzi bathtub and the room was lit up only by candlelight. I handed him his glass of wine and he kissed me before helping me into the tub. I stood until he was in the bathtub with me and we sat down together with my back to his chest. We sat in silence for a few moments before he complimented my tits, telling me just how perfect he thought they were. I knew they were perfect. I spent a lot of money paying for them to be perfect, but I loved hearing that he appreciated them.

After we got out of the bathtub, before even drying off, we stood making out with bubbles dripping down our bodies. His body looked so sexy covered in bubbles. I could stare at him naked all day long. Instead of drying off he, picked me up and carried me into his bedroom. After he lightly placed me on his bed, he got on top of me. It was the moment I had been waiting for! He slowly inserted his hard cock into my pussy and as it went in, my body melted with pleasure. I felt my pussy tightening up to hug his cock inside of me. He moved slowly in and out of me while he kissed my lips.

He sat back so he could watch his cock moving in and out of my pussy and I noticed he had a mirror on his ceiling. I could see him moving deeper and deeper inside of me and the sight of it turned me on even more.

He moved inside and out of me letting his cock get to know my pussy slowly and I loved every single thrust. I could feel the cum inside of my pussy covering his cock. I grabbed my breasts in pleasure and he smiled at me telling me how he loved when I grabbed my tits. He placed his thumb on my clit and moved it in a circular motion while he increased the speed of moving his cock in and out of my pussy. I moaned with pleasure and as he increased his speed more and more, I felt my pussy tightening until I reached the point where I couldn't hold back anymore. My pussy got so tight with pleasure that I came hard and loud. Immediately following my orgasm, he pulled out and came on my stomach.

We lay holding hands as we came down from our orgasm highs. I thought about how I loved what this man could do to my mind and body. I loved that I had found him at the perfect time, when I needed help getting out of my creativity funk. He's what I needed right now to inspire my creativity and explore sex. I hoped he'd want to stick around for a while.

Chase pulled his blanket up and wrapped his arms around me before saying, "I'd like for you to come out with me tomorrow night."

I replied, "Okay."

Chase said, "It's going to be a little different, though. I want you to come with a friend. It will be good to have someone with you while you see how it all works."

I asked, "How what works?"

He explained, "Well, I have an image of a playboy and when I am out, I am expected to act like a celebrity and a lot of women approach me. I want you to see it all to see if you would be comfortable with my projected Chicago industry lifestyle." I was interested in this situation. Did women just throw themselves at him all the time or something? I sure as hell threw myself at him. He continued on ... "If we end up dating, I'll worry about how we will project our image when the time comes, but for now I'd like to have you out with me just to see how my weekends go down."

I was extremely intrigued and wanted to see how his weekends went down, but I casually said, "Alright, I'll give it a go."

Friday night, as I got ready to go out as part of Chase Walker's entourage, I felt myself getting a little nervous. I had become less and less nervous around Chase, but I wasn't sure how I'd feel seeing swarms of women approach him. I realized that I was starting to feel for him, not just sexually and creatively desiring him, but falling for him. I had to go out and experience his lifestyle to see if I could handle it, though.

Even though Nikki thought Chase was a scumbag, I convinced her to come out with us. If something was free, she had a hard time saying no. I got a text from Chase an hour before he was going to pick Nikki and me up stating that there would be a film crew following us all night so I should dress my best. I wished I had known sooner so I could've gone to the trendy clothing boutique, Akira, for something new to wear. I decided a short and tight black dress was a safe bet.

Nikki came over and we waited for Chase and his entourage to pick us up. Chase sent me a text message when he was almost at my apartment so Nikki and I made our way downstairs. They pulled up in a big black SUV limo. When the driver opened the door, Chase got out and greeted me with a long, passionate kiss before saying, "I won't be able to kiss you all night and that makes me sad, but I assure you that when we get home tonight I will kiss every last inch of your body."

I was okay with not kissing while out, I wasn't much for public displays of affection anyway. We got into in the limo and Chase introduced Nikki and me to his friends, or as I call them, his "entourage." The film crew was in the van behind us. Basically, all I needed to know was that Chase always got out of the limo first and walked into the clubs first. We were just to follow and keep his table full. We were also not allowed to bring anyone in his VIP area. It all seemed simple enough.

Our first stop was at the night club Paris Club. After the limo pulled in front, we waited for the film crew to get out and prepare for Chase to get out of the limo. Chase's assistant, Mary, was riding with the film crew and she would send a text to Chase letting him know when to get out. Chase got out and Nikki and I were the next to follow. We walked right past the line and up the stairs. On our whole walk to our VIP area, there were cameras on Chase. It was exciting seeing all of the people stare at him and it turned me on knowing that I was the one that he'd be fucking that night.

We sat down at our VIP table and Nikki and I started drinking. I watched as new people constantly approached Chase. No wonder he enjoyed our quiet time together, he never had a moment alone. Every once in a while, Chase would look at me with a smile and wink. It made me happy knowing that he noticed my presence.

It was the same thing at the next two clubs

and I started to realize that we were really just props in Chase's world. I told myself it was okay that I was a prop because I was a prop who got free drinks and VIP service. I was getting a little tired and bored at the last place though and I couldn't wait to get home and get naked with Chase. Around 2 a.m., Chase came over by me, grabbed my hip and whispered in my ear, "You ready to get out of here? I want my dick inside of you."

I felt my pussy jump with excitement and butterflies spread through my body before I said with enthusiasm, "Yes, let's go!"

Chase waved his hand and everyone in the group got up to leave. We followed Chase out of the club and into the limo. The limo dropped us off at Chase's first. I would've liked to make sure Nikki got home safe first, but she hit it off with one of Chase's friends and I was pretty sure she'd be going home with him. When we got into the elevator at the Trump, Chase threw me up against the wall and kissed me passionately. I felt his hand move up under my tiny dress slowly caressing my pussy through my underwear. He said, "I can feel your pussy getting wet through your panties."

My pussy was wet. It was really wet and I just wanted his cock inside of me. No foreplay, I just wanted to get fucked hard. We got off the elevator and ran into his condo. Once in there he pulled my dress off fast and as soon as I was naked, I jumped up on him wrapping my legs around his body. He carried me into his bedroom and threw me onto his bed before saying, "I am going to fuck you so hard, you sexy whore!"

He read my mind! He pulled my panties off and dropped his pants. He came down to lie on top of me and I pulled off his shirt. He was so fucking sexy, especially when he was on top of me. He pushed his cock into my wet pussy, going deep right away. I tensed up with pleasure as he moved inside of me. He moved in and out deep and I could feel his cock getting harder until he pulled out and flipped my body over. I laid flat on my stomach, but lifted my hips up. He grabbed me from behind and slipped his cock back inside my pussy. His cock felt so fucking good inside of me. While he penetrated deeper and deeper inside of my pussy, he grabbed onto my hair and pulled it a little. I liked feeling the control he was taking over my body. It was turning me on and when he started calling me his whore, I felt my pussy tighten up faster. Words controlled my insides and the dirty talk got me so turned on that I could no longer hold back my orgasm. I tensed up in pleasure and released my orgasm. Soon after, I felt Chase pull out and cum all over my ass.

After Chase orgasmed, his lethargic body dropped down and lay on my back. He whispered in my ear, "I just love fucking you."

I smiled and said, "I love when you fuck me, too."

After several minutes of catching our breaths, we laid our heads on the pillows looking at each other. He asked, "What did you think about tonight?"

I responded nonchalantly, "It was fine."

He asked, "Fine?"

"It was hot seeing you as a celebrity."

"Did it bother you that women were approaching me?"

"Nah, I mean, look at me. Why would you want any of that when you could have all this?" I let out a little laugh after I said those words.

He laughed and said, "I couldn't agree more."

I asked, "Do you have to do that every weekend?"

"Pretty much, well at least for the next couple of months while we are filming. It's part of our marketing to make me into a local celebrity."

"Why do you need to be a local celebrity?"

"Men buy my program or hire me as a personal coach to be more successful with women. Being out at the clubs is advertising in itself because women are constantly throwing themselves at me and the guys that come out with me."

"True, a lot of women do approach you. Don't you get sick of it?"

"I can't because I want my company to be successful. I do know that it makes me appreciate the alone time I've had with you lately."

I smiled. "Going out with you is so different from what I am used to. I'm a writer so everything I do is behind the scenes. The biggest celebrity I've been is at book signings and readings, which is usually only thirty to forty people in a bookstore."

"If we continued dating, would you be okay with this lifestyle?"

My stomach dropped a little when I realized we were having some sort of "future talk." I said, "Right now, your lifestyle doesn't bother me, but I did notice myself looking away when women were talking to you. I don't know if I'd want to do this type of thing every single weekend. I would want to go out and do my own thing sometimes with my friends."

Chase smiled at me as he asked, "Then come home to me?"

"Yeah, I mean if you are cool with that. It's just that I felt like a prop sometimes tonight and I might get bored doing that every weekend."

"I understand. If you and I work out, would you be okay with a celebrity-like lifestyle?"

"Hmm, I've never really thought about that."

"I know it's down the road and for now I want to keep us private, but it's something for you to think about."

A few weeks went by and not a day passed without Chase telling me how beautiful and wonderful I was. I was slowly getting used to Chase's lifestyle and feeling more and more for him with each day. We spent nights alone during the week and I'd go out with him and his entourage one night on the weekends. I went with Chase to watch him record a couple of his podcasts and I got to sit in the audience when he was a guest on the Chicago morning talk show *Windy City Live*. My favorite part about it was that I was becoming his sounding board. He would run his new ideas and theories past me first. I had completely let go of the idea of doing an article on him. Rumors were circulating about us in the industry and I didn't want to publish something and end up getting questioned about it. I didn't need to do an article on him to feel good about my writing anymore. I was finishing up my novel and he was connecting me with new people and places I could pitch for articles.

We were really getting to know each other's bodies and starting to explore more with each other sexually. I loved the feeling of desire I had for him and each time we fucked it increased more and more. He knew how to pleasure my body and he seemed like he never wanted to stop learning how to pleasure it in different ways. Chase appreciated my body and me and consistently told me how much he did, it was no wonder my confidence skyrocketed after I met him.

When I went to his house one Tuesday night, he asked me if I wanted to go to Las Vegas with him that weekend. When I told him that I'd love to go, I realized that I was really starting to enjoy dating someone with money and fame. I had never dated a guy who said, "Hey, let's go out of town this weekend!" Well, I guess I went with my ex Tim to Jamaica and another ex Ryan to Los Angeles, but those were all planned out trips and I paid my own way.

On Thursday afternoon, Chase picked me up in a limo to head to the airport. I asked, "So am I just a part of your entourage this weekend?"

Chase responded, "No, you are going to be my girl by my side. I'm really only a local celebrity so not many people outside of Chicago know me. I am all yours except when I have to go speak Saturday at a seminar."

"Can I come to the seminar and watch you speak?"

"Of course, I'd love to have you see me speak."

When we checked into the Hard Rock Hotel, we got naked as soon as we got into our suite. We spent the entire plane ride bouncing ideas off of each other. I talked to him about my book ending and he talked to me about new theories, podcasts, and article ideas. Chase and I talking creatively turned me on. He kissed me passionately the moment we walked into our suite and he pulled my shirt off as we made our way toward the bedroom, but he stopped and started leading me toward the window. He pushed my back up against the window and kissed me down my chest and stomach before pulling my pants and underwear off. Once they were off, he looked up smiling at me, spun my body around and started licking my pussy from behind. I spread my legs apart for easier access. My tits pushed up against the window while I looked at the little people down below and enjoyed him teasing my pussy. I could feel the cum dripping out of my pussy and into his mouth.

After a few minutes, he turned me back around, dropped his pants and pushed his hard cock inside of me. I wrapped one leg around his back as he fucked me hard against the window. He knew exactly what spots to hit inside of me and I moaned loud. I said, "Give it to me harder with that big cock!"

He pushed deeper inside of me and asked, "Do you like when my cock is inside of you?"

"I love when your cock is inside of me. Harder!"

He pushed deeper and faster and said, "Oh, yeah, baby, I feel your pussy getting tighter."

"My pussy loves your cock."

"Cum for me baby, cum all over my cock. I want to feel you orgasm while I am inside of you."

His words were so sexy and my pussy got really tight. When I saw him bite his lip, I couldn't control it anymore and my body tensed up before I released an orgasm. Once my body began to relax after my orgasm, Chase pulled out and came all over the window. It was fucking hot. He took a deep breath then leaned in and kissed me softly before saying, "You are so fucking beautiful."

Nobody has ever made me feel as beautiful or wanted as Chase did. He was always looking at me with admiring eyes or telling me how wonderful I was. He was always appreciating me not only for my looks, but for my mind, too. I felt like he couldn't get enough of me and I knew I couldn't get enough of him.

The next morning after breakfast, Chase and I went down to the pool. His assistant, a cameraman, and soundman would be arriving that afternoon to get some footage for his reality show pilot, but for now it was just us. A VIP host walked us to our cabana and as we walked holding hands, a girl stopped us. I immediately thought she was stopping us to talk to Chase, but to my surprise she complimented my bathing suit. Chase said to the girl, "Isn't she beautiful?" He then lifted my hand up with his and told me to do a spin to show off my bathing suit. I loved feeling that he was proud to have me by his side and it felt nice to be able to act like a couple in a social setting.

Chase and I mingled with people, but also snuck away into our cabana for time alone. When we were in the cabana, I suggested we go behind the cabana and fuck. He looked at me, smiled and asked if I was serious. I told him I'd just pull my swimsuit bottom to the side. I saw his cock getting hard at the thought of a quickie behind the cabana and my pussy starting getting wet knowing he was turned on. I said, "Come on, let's do it! We'll be fast!"

Chase went behind the cabana to check out

the situation. When he saw it was clear, he signaled me to sneak back with him. There wasn't much room for us to maneuver, but it was very private. Chase pulled his cock out and slipped it inside of my pussy from behind. He fucked me fast and after just a couple of minutes, he pulled out and came on some rocks. I didn't get off, but I was high off the possibility of getting caught and knowing that he got off. I walked back into our cabana first and then he followed. I don't think anyone noticed, but I didn't give a fuck if they did.

We sat down in the cabana and relaxed for a few minutes sipping on our drinks. As he recovered from his orgasm, I told him I wanted to start a journal of our sexual experiences. He puckered up his lips for a second like he was thinking and then told me he thought it was a great idea. He thought it would be fun for us to do the journal together and I agreed. He then turned to me and asked, "Would you be open to a threesome?"

I had never thought about doing a threesome before. There were times where I found women attractive, but I never thought about actually being intimate with one. Maybe he was talking about having one with another man, though. I asked, "With a man or woman?"

Chase said with a tone indicating that it wasn't even a question, "A woman, of course."

"Well, umm ... I'd have to think about it more."

"You do that."

His assistant, cameraman, and soundman came by our cabana and the camera was rolling. All of a sudden, Chase was the talk of the pool and I felt like a prop again. There was nothing I could do about it, but let him do his thing. Luckily, it only lasted for a little while and then Chase said he was heading upstairs for a nap before dinner. He suggested I join him.

We got upstairs and had a quickie before we took a nap. His alarm went off at 7pm and we got up to shower and get ready. We showered together where he washed me and then fingered me until I came. His fingers, tongue, cock and mind were so magical. We put on some music and danced around while we got ready. We met his crew downstairs and then headed to dinner.

After dinner, we had a table at a night club. The crew wasn't filming so we were all enjoying a fun night. I got to enjoy the nightlife with non-celebrity Chase for the first time and it felt great. We walked around, we mingled, and we danced. I felt like I had a boyfriend even though we hadn't talked about that sort of thing yet. This vacation was turning out great.

The next morning Chase's phone alarm went off at 9am. As usual, he didn't budge. I was wide-awake from the blaring noise so I decided to go under the covers and put my mouth on his cock to wake him up pleasantly. I sucked on his cock from under the sheets until he got off. Once I had a mouth full of cum, I swallowed and appeared from under the sheets. He smiled at me when my head popped out and then grabbed my face to kiss me. After he kissed me he said, "I'm going to marry you some day."

My heart dropped and tingles spread through my body. Did he just mention marriage? We hadn't even talked about being boyfriend and girlfriend, let alone marriage. Maybe he was drunk from the night before. Maybe I was taking his words too seriously. I didn't know how to respond so I just smiled and kissed him like a giddy little girl.

Chase showered and left to go to the hotel Bellagio for the seminar. He wasn't speaking until 1pm, but had to be there early. I went back to sleep for a couple hours and then met him at the seminar right before he went on stage to speak. I sat with Mary in the back of the room while Chase spoke to a group of at least one hundred men. I felt so proud of him up there speaking like it was no big deal. He looked so confident and didn't look the least bit nervous. I admired that. I was not good at public speaking at all. He looked so sexy and all I could think about was being naked with him eating my pussy. I should've been paying attention to what he was saying, but I found myself fantasizing about him fucking me on and behind the stage.

After the seminar, Chase said he needed to stay at Bellagio for a bit, but that there was a cabana reserved back at the Hard Rock pool under his name. He told me to go back and relax and he would be there soon. Mary, the cameraman, and the soundman stayed with Chase so I was on my own. I got back to the hotel, put on my swimsuit and grabbed my iPad. I figured I could do some reading down by the pool while I waited for Chase. When I got down by the pool, the VIP host showed me to a cabana and I ordered a fruity drink. I was sitting and reading for a couple hours when a guy invited himself into my cabana. He was pretty good-looking, but nowhere near as hot as Chase. I was bored so when he hit on me, I humored him and flirted back a little. His name was Tony and he was a few years my junior, but after talking a bit it turns out he was from San Diego and used to date my cousin. Small world.

Chase came back from the seminar and as he was approaching the cabana, he saw me talking to Tony. He looked a little concerned, but remained cool. I introduced them and explained how Tony and I were connected. Chase talked with Tony for a few minutes and then Tony left. Once Tony left, Chase crawled onto the chair with me, gave me a big kiss and told me how beautiful I was. I told him how sexy he looked on stage and that I tried to figure out a way for us to fuck behind it.

We went out that night, but only for a couple hours. We got Mary, the cameraman, and soundman set up at a table at a club and then we left. On our way back to the Hard Rock, we stopped at a strip club. It was pretty early to be at a Las Vegas strip club, but we thought it would be fun. We "stripper shopped" and pretended like we were looking for a girl to have a threesome with. With each girl that came by, we told one another what our preferences were with their bodies and mannerisms. It was actually a turn on. Until this weekend, I never thought about getting intimate with a woman, but with each stripper that came by, I realized how attractive women are. I wasn't sure how I would handle it logistically if I were to become intimate with a woman, but the fantasy of it was fun.

We "stripper shopped" for a little over an hour and then Chase said to me, "These girls just don't do it for me. I want to take you back to our room and have my way with your body."

I grabbed his hand and said, "Let's go!"

As we walked down the street toward the Hard Rock, we passed a sex shop and I suggested we go in. Chase laughed and followed me in. When we got in there, we both had smiles on our faces. There were so many fun things that could help us explore each other. From games to chains, we picked out about ten items to take back to the hotel suite with us. When we got back in our suite, I immediately went into the bathroom to put on the edible lingerie I picked out while Chase mixed us up some drinks. When I walked out of the bathroom he looked at me and said, "You have the perfect little body. Fuck these toys! Let me fuck you right now!"

I waved my index finger back and forth telling him no. I wanted to explore these new items with him. We sat down on the couch and looked at the items we had purchased. I picked up the bullet vibrator and told Chase to take his pants off. He took them off faster than I have ever seen anyone take off pants before. I told him to sit back down and I put my mouth on his cock. I felt it increase in size by the second. Once he was fully erect I turned on the vibrating bullet and held it up against his balls while I sucked on his cock.

I didn't finish him off. I wanted to cum together. He said, "Quit teasing me, baby."

I responded, "We've only just begun."

Chase smiled at me and then stood up,

instructing me to sit down on the couch. I did as he requested and he ran the feather teaser we bought lightly around my body. I could feel the cum gathering on my edible panties. After a few minutes of light teasing of my body, he began to lick around my breasts before calmly chewing off the edible bra. Once he had the bra off, he licked my nipples before blowing on them, which brought me so much pleasure. He worked his way down to my pussy and used force to pull the edible underwear off. He said he was getting anxious to taste me.

Chase licked my pussy gently then used the bullet vibrator to tease me around my clit and labia. It sent vibrations of pleasure through my body. I loved his gentle touch. After teasing me with licks and vibrations, he held out his hand and escorted me to the bedroom where he handcuffed me and blindfolded me, telling me I had been a bad girl for not sucking his cock until he finished. I liked being his bad girl and I was ready for him to punish me. He bent me over the side of the bed and licked my pussy from behind for a few moments before spanking my ass and reminding me how bad I was. After a few spankings I felt his cock penetrate my pussy. The initial penetration was always so pleasurable. I felt him slowly move deep before grabbing my hips and fucking me hard. He then spun me around and threw me on the bed. He placed my handcuffed hands over my head and said, "You are so fucking bad, you hot little bitch! I am going to fuck you hard until you cum all over my cock."

I screamed out, "Punish me until I cum!"

Chase grabbed my feet and spread my legs

wide, wider than I had ever gotten them to go when I did the splits. It hurt, but it hurt so good. He continued holding my legs spread apart as he fucked me deep, so deep that I could feel it in my lungs. He was hitting my G-spot head on and hard. Each time he hit it, I felt my pussy get tighter and tighter with pleasure. He said, "Tighten that pussy up for me. I want to feel your pussy grab onto my cock hard."

I was close to coming and I yelled out, "I'm going to cum."

He pulled his cock out and said, "You aren't going to cum until I say you can cum, you whore."

I screamed back, "Put your cock back inside of me and make me cum, now!"

He rolled me over and slapped my ass three times saying, "I'll tell you when you can cum." He then penetrated me again and asked, "How bad do you want to cum?"

"I need to cum, now! Let me cum Chase, I promise I'll be a good girl."

"Say please."

"Please."

"Louder."

I screamed, "Please!" and after I said it, I felt my entire body get tense then release in orgasm. As soon as I finished, Chase pulled out and I felt him cum on my ass.

I lifted the blindfold off my eyes and Chase crashed down on the bed to lie next to me. I watched his sweaty body breathe heavily as he recovered from fucking me. He looked so sexy. I just smiled at him feeling so good that this man was fucking me. He smiled back and said, "I just love fucking you."

DATING CHASE WALKER

Back from Las Vegas, I spent most of my time rigorously working on my novel. I was feeling so inspired that I couldn't get the words I wanted to write out fast enough. I knew the ending of my story and I so badly wanted to get there just like I so badly wanted to cum when Chase fucked me.

On Wednesday night, I went to dinner with Nikki and Bree. They were giving me shit because I was spending all of my time with Chase. I promised myself I'd never be that girl that ignored all of her friends once she got involved with a guy. While we were at dinner, a girl approached our table. She looked like she wanted to bitch slap one of us. When she got to the table, she looked me straight in the eye and asked, "Are you dating Chase Walker?"

Chase and I hadn't discussed our relationship so I just said, "I'm seeing him."

"Well, girl, you better get yourself checked out. My friend Ashley used to date him and he gave her syphilis."

My stomach dropped. I didn't know how to respond. Was this girl serious? I just said, "Okay."

With attitude she said, "I just thought I should tell you girl to girl."

I said with confusion, "Umm, thank you?"

"I'm being serious. I'm not some crazy

bitch. My friend Ashley," she pointed at a table behind her, "heard you guys are dating and we wanted to warn you. He's fucking dirty. Be careful."

I asked, "When did they date?"

"Well, they more or less just hooked up a few times a couple months ago."

"Thanks for telling me."

"No prob."

The random girl walked away and Nikki said, "I warned you he was a fucking scumbag."

I said, "Isn't syphilis treatable?"

Bree chimed in, "Yeah, it just takes some antibiotics. If he was on them long enough before you guys met then you should be good."

Nikki said, "Go get checked out, anyway. Who knows if he gave you something else?"

I was a bit freaked out because I had not been careful with Chase at all. In fact, we never used a condom once. I asked, "Should I ask him about this?"

Nikki said I should ask Chase right away, but Nikki always loved drama. Bree told me I should go get checked out first and then deal with the results if something came up. I decided to take Bree's advice and called to make an appointment with my gynecologist the next morning. Unfortunately, I couldn't get in to see him until the next week so I had to keep quiet about what had happened that weekend. It affected my sex with Chase because it was all I could think about when his cock was inside of me. I kept visioning little syphilis alien looking things going in and attacking my vagina. Chase noticed I had been a bit off and I tried to blame it on me being anxious about my book.

I arrived at my gynecologist's office right on time Tuesday morning, but after signing in, I waited over twenty minutes before a nurse came out to get me. I'm convinced it is standard practice for doctors to make you sit and wait because I have never once gone to a doctor's appointment and been called back at my scheduled time. After the nurse finally called my name, I followed her back to the exam room stopping at the scale, where she noted I had lost weight since my last visit. Once in the exam room, she took my blood pressure and asked when the first day of my last menstrual cycle was. I checked the Period Tracker application on my phone and told her the date. She asked all of the standard medical questions then handed me a gown, telling me to get fully undressed and the doctor would be right in. I did as instructed and then waited patiently for Dr. White to come in.

A good ten minutes passed before Dr. White came in, but I filled the time fiddling with the plastic vagina on the counter and checking Facebook on my phone. When the doctor came in, I set my phone down on the table and he shook my hand. Dr. White was always so bubbly. I guess looking at vaginas all day served him well. I don't know if I would want to marry a gynecologist. You'd think at some point he'd get sick of looking at vaginas all day. Did he ever go home at night and his wife would be looking all sexy, but he would say, "If I see one more damn vagina today, I think I might...?" I know if I had to deal with something day in and day out, I wouldn't want to have to deal with it at night when I was off from work.

But then again, I never could get sick of dealing with words. Frustrated, yes, but sick of them, never. Maybe vaginas were to him what words were to me.

Dr. White threw some small talk at me before getting down to business by asking if I was sexually active. I said, "Yes."

He asked, "Are you in a monogamous relationship?"

I replied with hesitation, "Err, well we just started seeing each other umm ... like two months ago."

He asked, "You are still taking the pill, right? And using protection?"

"The pill, yes, but I haven't been so good about protection. That's why I am here. I want all the STI tests."

"Are you worried you may have contracted something specific?"

"Well, I heard a rumor about him having syphilis in the past."

"What did he say about the rumor?"

"I didn't bring it up. I figured I'd get tested and then talk to him if there was an issue."

Dr. White shook his head at me, "You should always use protection until you and your partner have discussed being monogamous and have both been tested."

I felt like a kid who had just gotten into trouble. I knew better, but I went ahead with it anyway. God, I hoped my vagina was clean. Having a sexually transmitted infection conversation with Chase scared me. I lay back on the exam table and while Dr. White gave me a breast exam, I told him that I got my tan in Las Vegas. He then told me about his trip to Las

Vegas a few years back where he ended up winning $10,000. While he was telling me the story, I realized I didn't gamble once while I was in Las Vegas. Usually, I would at least play a few slot machines to test my luck.

After my breast exam, Dr. White had me scoot down to the end of the exam table and instructed me to put my legs in the stirrups. I hated this part. I looked down and saw him holding the metal thing that cranked crotches open. I decided staring at the ceiling was a better option. I felt him crank my crotch open and then he said, "Relax."

How could I relax when I was being violated? I kept saying over and over in my head, "Please be over. Please be over," but then a nurse swung open the door to the exam room and yelled out, "Doctor, we need you right away!"

Dr. White pulled off his gloves and as he was exiting the exam room he said, "Sit tight for a moment, Audrey."

What the fuck? Seriously, he was leaving me here with my crotch wide open? What if a spider crawled in there? After about three of the longest minutes of my life, I heard my phone ringing. I could tell it was Chase by the ringtone. I wasn't going to answer, but I badly needed a distraction from the cold air entering my cooter. I stretched my arm onto the table next to me and answered the phone, "Hello."

Chase said in a very chipper tone, "Good morning, my beautiful baby. How are you today?"

I quietly responded, "I'm at the gynecologist right now."

He asked, "What for?"

What for? I wanted to say getting my crotch checked out because word on the street is that you are a huge man slut, but I held it in and simply said, "For my annual tune-up."

"Keep that pussy pretty."

"Well, right now I am sprawled out on the table with my crotch cranked open. The doctor ran out of the room for an emergency."

"He just left you in there? I'd love to be there to look inside your beautiful pussy and tell it how wonderful it is." I know Chase was trying to be charming, but it was a total turn off. There was nothing remotely sexy about your crotch being cranked open at the gyno-office. I didn't know how to react so I said nothing. He must've felt the awkward silence and changed the subject by saying, "Well, come by my office after you are finished there. I want you to watch me record my next podcast because I want your feedback."

I said, "Okay," but then Dr. White walked back in and I said, "I gotta go," before hanging up the phone. Dr. White put a new pair of gloves on while he apologized for the disruption. I wanted to ask what happened because I am nosy, but I left it alone. I felt him stick some Q-Tips up my cooter and then he finally took out the vagina stretcher and I felt a sense of relief. That sense of relief didn't last, though. About a minute later, he shoved his jelly-covered fingers up my crotch and poked around. It was as uncomfortable as the first time my first boyfriend fingered me. I hated coming here. Before I left the nurse came in and drew my blood for the remainder of the sexually transmitted infection tests I requested. What a shitty day.

The next week Dr. White's nurse called me and told me I had a clean bill of health. I was relieved, but I started to think that it was time to bring up the monogamous conversation with Chase. I wasn't sleeping with anyone else and I was pretty sure he wasn't either, but the sexually transmitted infection scare made me think that I needed to be responsible and have the dreaded talk. I just needed the balls and the right situation to bring it up.

A few days later, after a long round of cock sucking, pussy banging, and ass spanking we were lying on Chase's bed and he looked at me and said, "My God, you are just so fucking beautiful. I really am going to marry you some day."

This was the second time he had said to me that he was going to marry me and I felt it was a good time to find out if he was seriously thinking that or just charming my panties off. I said, "I want to talk to you about something."

Chase said, "Uh oh, that doesn't sound good."

"It's not bad. It's just that it has been a couple months and we haven't been careful about using protection. I guess, err, umm ... am I the only girl you are sleeping with?"

Chase responded, "Absolutely, I have not slept with any girls since the first time we had sex."

With a little bit of relief, I said, "Okay."

Chase asked, "Are you fucking anyone else?"

I said, "Nope, I am only fucking you."

Chase went on to explain himself further by saying, "I was dating a couple girls when we first started seeing each other, but after we had sex, I broke ties with them. There was something about you, so I wanted to spend all my time exploring you."

I started to wonder if one of the girls Chase was dating was that Ashley girl that had her friend approach me at the bar. Maybe he did have syphilis and he was waiting to finish his antibiotics so he didn't sleep with me right away. I didn't say anything about Ashley or the syphilis though, I just said, "Alright, I just wanted to get that conversation out of the way."

"We are all good, baby. Now, would you like me to give you a foot massage?"

I accepted the foot massage and while he was massaging my feet, I don't know why, but I decided to ask, "So, are we a couple?"

Chase replied, "If you want to label it, yes, we are a couple."

I asked, "Do you want to label it?"

"I am okay with labeling it if that's what you need."

"I don't need the label, but I guess I was just wondering if this is going anywhere."

"It has the possibility to go anywhere at this point. Let's just enjoy each day and let it evolve naturally."

"So why do you tell me you're going to marry me someday?"

"Because I am."

"How do you know that?"

"I have the ability to see the future, Audrey. You are my dream girl and some day I am going to marry you."

His words made me smile. It felt good hear Chase call me his "dream girl." I decided to slowly move in for a kiss to end this conversation. I was ready to fuck again.

I was hard at work attempting to write the perfect ending to my book when I got a call from Chase. I was in a creative writing zone so I decided to ignore his call. A few minutes later, Chase called again, but I ignored it again. I needed to finish my book while I was on a roll. When he called for the third time in five minutes I began to worry so I picked up the phone, "Hello."

Chase asked, "Hi, beautiful, how are you?"

I responded, "Hard at work on my book. Can I call you later?"

"I need you to come over."

"I can later tonight. I want to finish this writing, it's important."

"I really need you here now to help me with some stuff. Can't you write later?"

"I can, but I am having a great creative flow and I want to finish the story."

Chase had a bit of an attitude when he said, "Fine, I'll figure this stuff out myself. Good luck writing."

I liked that Chase wanted and needed me, but I was a little annoyed that he had an attitude about me making my writing a priority. I brushed it off and got back to work. That evening, when I finished the final chapter in my book, I stood up from my desk and danced around my apartment with excitement.

I finally finished the book I had been working on for months! I wanted to celebrate and I wanted to celebrate with Chase since he was the one that started to make my mind and body feel alive again. I called Chase, but he didn't answer so I left a very enthusiastic message on his voice mail telling him I had finished my book and I wanted to celebrate!

I danced around my apartment some more, hoping Chase would call me back soon. After fifteen minutes of dancing and no call back, I was out of breath and I decided to call Nikki to tell her the good news. I was so proud of myself and excited about my story that I had to share it with someone. Nikki screamed in the phone with enthusiasm and asked to read my manuscript as soon as possible. I assured her that once I read through it a couple times and finished all my adjustments, she'd get a copy. I always loved Nikki's feedback with my writing. She was brutally honest.

Nikki suggested we meet at the old bar we frequented between our apartments for a celebration drink. I was in. I hadn't eaten anything except a powdered donut all day so I was ready to grab some food, too. Since it was just a local bar that we went to often, I didn't dress up for the occasion. I wore a t-shirt, yoga pants, and a hat to cover up my naked face. I had no intention of socializing with anyone. I just wanted to celebrate and be goofy with Nikki.

After eating, Nikki ordered a round of shots for us. A few minutes later, another round of shots arrived at our table from a table of guys. We cheered the men at the table and took the shots down like pros. Unfortunately, the guys must've thought that us accepting the shots they sent over was an invitation to come over and join us. The guys came over and Nikki lit up because one of the guys had a bald head and a sleeve of tattoos. Bald men with tattoos were Nikki's weakness. She loved all types of men, but could never deny a bald, tattooed man.

It turned out that the guys were pretty fun. I told them about finishing my book and they seemed sincerely excited for me. One of the guys was an intellectual type so we hit it off by talking about classic literature. It was fun getting into the words of some of the most famous authors while feeling a little drunk. I didn't encounter many people who were as passionate about words as me.

After my sixth shot and third drink, I decided it was time to call it a night. I told Nikki I was going to head home, but she insisted I stay for one more drink. I had one more drink and left her at the bar with Mr. Bald Tattoo. On my way home, I checked my phone and I had fourteen missed calls and six text messages from Chase. I called Chase back and when he answered he said, "Where have you been?"

I think I slurred a little when I said, "With Nikki, celebrating my book."

"I've been calling you and I wanted to celebrate with you. Why didn't you answer my calls?"

I felt myself slur some more when I said, "My phone was in my purse."

He asked with an angry tone, "Are you drunk?"

I concentrated trying not to slur when I said, "A tiny bit."

"What were you doing that you couldn't check your phone?"

"I was just chatting with some people."

"Guys?"

"Yeah, Nikki found this bald, tattooed guy. She's still at the bar with him."

"And you?"

"And me, what?"

"Were you talking with guys?"

"There was this one intellectual guy that I talked about literature with."

Chase raised his voice a little when he said, "You just had a conversation with me about being exclusive and then you go out talking with a guy all night ignoring my calls."

I didn't like him raising his voice at me, but I responded calmly saying, "I didn't mean to ignore your calls."

"How do you think that makes me feel? I wanted to be celebrating with you."

"I called you earlier."

"I know; I called you back as soon as I could. I was recording a video."

"Okay, I'm fine with that. We can celebrate tomorrow."

"Whatever. We should've been celebrating tonight together. I should go, I'm pretty heated."

"Don't be upset, Chase. I was just down the street at a local tavern. It was no big deal."

"Well, it should've been a big deal and I would've made it a big deal if I were there."

"I know you would've. Tomorrow."

"Whatever. I'm going to go cool down."

Chase hung up the phone. I was confused at the way he was acting. Was he really upset I went out without him? He was making this about him and I kind of felt like he was being a little controlling. Maybe his feelings were just hurt so that's why he was upset. I decided to flag down a cab and head over to his place. I sent him a text telling him I was coming over. I was drunk and a bit horny so I might as well make-up with him and get laid. I signed in at the front desk in his building and when I arrived at his floor, he wasn't waiting by the elevators like he had done every time in the past. I lightly knocked on his door and he yelled, "Come in."

When I got inside, he just sat on his couch, quiet. He didn't say hello and he didn't tell me I was beautiful. I was experiencing angry Chase for the first time and, in a twisted way, it turned me on. It felt like a challenge to get him to praise me like he usually did. I walked closer to him and, on my walk toward him, I pulled my shirt off. When I got close to him, I spread my legs around him and got on his lap. I lifted his face up to kiss him and noticed he had been crying. I wasn't sure why he was crying over this. I kissed him and after I pulled away from the kiss, I wiped his tears and said, "I'm sorry if I upset you."

He rested his head on my breasts and said, "I've had a really crappy day, Audrey. All I wanted to do was to talk to you and you didn't even answer my calls."

I sincerely said, "I'm sorry I didn't answer your calls. I am here for you now. Tell me your woes."

Chase sort of whined when he said, "I should've been out with you celebrating and you ignored me."

"I didn't intentionally ignore you."

"Why wouldn't you check your phone for three hours?"

"I was just talking to people."

"I check my phone for your calls and texts every single time I get the chance."

"I'm sorry. How about I suck your cock? Will that make you feel better?"

Chase let out a little chuckle and said, "I don't think it will hurt."

I got off his lap and got down on my knees before pulling his pants off. His cock was soft and had a bit of a stench to it, but I proceeded anyway. I fondled and sucked his cock until it got hard. Once it was hard, I looked up at him and smiled. He smiled back as he wiped a tear off his cheek. As I slobbered all over his knob for several minutes, I kept wondering why he was crying. What happened today that was so stressful that it brought him to tears? It was an inappropriate time to ask as my mouth was full of cock so I decided to continue on with sucking his cock and then I would ask for details after he came. He might be in a better mood after an orgasm anyway. I was sucking his cock fast when Chase said, "I want to fuck you," before lifting me up and escorting me to his bedroom.

When we got in his bedroom, he pulled off my pants and I lifted off his shirt. He then pushed me on the bed, got on top of me and penetrated me. The initial penetration of sex never got old. In fact, any penetration from Chase never got old. My pussy fit like a glove over his cock. As he was fucking me, he looked at me and said, "You are just so fucking beautiful. I am so glad you are all mine."

After Chase spoke those words, I saw another tear drop from his eye and land on my chest. Why was he crying? I was distracted thinking again about what had happened to him during the day, but I tried to ignore my thoughts because I wanted an orgasm. I cleared my mind and looked at his hot body instead of his teary face. My God, was he sexy. The way the muscles on his arms flexed over my body when he fucked me was so hot. I got in the orgasm zone and a few minutes later felt my body tighten up and release with pleasure. Right after I came, Chase pulled out and came all over my stomach. He then lay down next to me and pulled me into his arms real tight before he said, "I love you."

I was a little taken back at first because it was the first time he told me he loved me, but I knew I had intense feelings for him so I said, "I love you, too."

He asked, "Really, do you mean that?"

Why was he acting so insecure? I said, "Of course I mean it. Why would I tell you that I love you if I didn't mean it?"

"I'm sorry. I had a rough day and I am feeling insecure. I got my ass handed to me today. It just seems like everything went wrong."

"Just take a few deeps breaths. Today is almost over and tomorrow you can start fresh."

Chase asked, "Can we just lay here with me holding you for a few minutes?"

I cuddled into his arms as I said, "I wouldn't

want to be anywhere else."

About two minutes later, I heard Chase snoring. I had no idea he was such an emotional being. He always projected himself as so calm and in control. I wasn't used to emotional men, my father only showed the emotions of happiness or anger, so this kind of emotion from a man was new to me. I liked that he was opening up to me so much and that I got to see a side of him that most people never would. I listened to his snoring for a few minutes, but even with his body heat I started feeling cold. I tried to slowly and gently move out of his arms and once I broke free he woke up and asked, "Where are you going?"

I whispered, "I am just going to head home. You get some sleep."

Chase said, "Please stay with me tonight, Audrey."

I responded, "I don't have any stuff here."

"Please, I need to feel you next to me."

I guess I really didn't need anything from my place tonight, anyway. I crawled back onto the bed and Chase moved his head up by the pillow. I pulled the blanket over us and he pulled me into his arms tight. I cuddled into him and closed my eyes. A few minutes later I was asleep.

I woke up the next morning to Chase's hard dick poking my back. It sent butterflies through my body. I felt his hands rubbing up and down my side and I knew I was about to get laid. I turned over and Chase got on top of me. I had barely opened my eyes so everything was still a bit blurry, but I could see the outline of his sexy body. When he penetrated me, I am pretty sure

I thanked God for sex and then thanked God again for giving me the pleasure of sex with Chase's beautiful cock.

After we finished fucking, Chase seemed to have kicked his depressed mood completely and was a ball of happiness. I attached to his good mood even though I felt a bit hungover. Chase asked what I wanted to do during the morning and I told him I should get home and start the editing process of my book. I always had five rounds of editing I did myself and with friends before I sent a finished story to my agent. Chase insisted I stay for breakfast and I agreed to, but then when I tried to leave after breakfast, he insisted I stay longer. I wanted to leave because I felt like I had to take a shit and I didn't like pooping at other people's places, especially when I am at risk for the alcohol shits. Plus, I really needed to brush my teeth and wash my face so I told him I didn't have anything at his place and needed to get home to shower up.

Chase kept insisting I stay, though, providing me with an extra toothbrush of his and telling me I could shower there. He was rather convincing so I went into the bathroom, brushed my teeth, turned on the shower and took a shit while the water was running. I hoped the smell would be gone by the time I was finished showering. When I came out of the bathroom Chase said, "I don't think I will ever be able to get over how beautiful you are."

His words made me glad I stayed. I felt a rush of butterflies run through my body, and my face got flushed. I asked, "So, what are we doing? Why did you want me to stay?"

Chase responded, "Let's go for a walk. I need you to be my sounding board as I practice for a seminar I am doing."

He wanted me to stay to be his sounding board? I loved hearing his ideas and connecting with him, but it's like he didn't realize how important editing my book was. Fresh air would do my hangover good, so I convinced myself that I should be there for him and that I could work on editing my book that night. The walk was nice and when we got back, we fucked. I figured I was safe to leave because I had been his sounding board for over an hour on our walk, but then he pulled out his computer to show me some more new ideas. One of the ideas was to have me start writing for his company. He wanted to implement a new promotional idea called "Chasers." Basically, he wanted to create a big female fan base because if you put beautiful women into the mix, men come naturally. He would build a group of women who would talk about his company, post sexy photos through his website, and write for his website. He wanted me to be his first female writer that focused on sex from a woman's point of view. I did like writing and I really liked writing about sex. I told him I'd think about it, but that finishing my book came first so I needed to get home and work on editing.

He finally stopped insisting I stay and agreed to dismiss me. He had just bought a fancy new car so he drove me home. On the way home, he told me he would pick me up at 10 p.m. to go out that night. I was unaware we had made plans and hoped to stay home to edit. He said it was really important to him that I come

out with him and his friends tonight so I agreed.
I was such a pushover for him.

After our night out, I went home with
Chase. We were a little tipsy and made out in
the elevator. I still felt so electrified when he
touched me. Sure, there were days that it
wasn't as thrilling as other days, but most of
the time I thrived off the high that his touch
gave me. When we walked into his condo, I
started pulling his clothes off immediately, but
he stopped me and said he had a surprise for
me. I loved surprises and couldn't wait to see
what he had in store for me. I figured it was
something sexual like lingerie, a sex swing, or
maybe even a little whip. He escorted me into
his bedroom and walked up to his dresser. He
opened a drawer and it was empty. He said,
"I've made space for you to leave stuff so you
can stay here more often and feel comfortable."

It was no sex swing to satisfy how horny I
was, but it was a gesture that made my heart
melt. I went in to kiss him to thank him and to
get back to getting naked. He went on to say,
"There's more," and he walked me into his
gigantic closet where he had opened up space
for me.

I asked, "How much stuff do you want me to
leave here?"

"As much as you want, but there's more."
We continued walking into his bathroom, where
he had cleared out a drawer for me. In it were
all the skincare, hair care, and other toiletries
that he had bought for me to keep there. I
couldn't believe he remembered all those
products. He had been to my apartment a few
times, but I wouldn't think a guy would pay

attention to products. I know I had no idea what products he used.

I reached in for another thank-you kiss. I was smitten with his gesture, but still horny so I pushed until our gratitude kiss turned into a passionate "I'm going to fuck you" kiss. We undressed right there in the bathroom and then he turned me around and penetrated my pussy from behind. *Oh, the ecstasy of the initial penetration.* As he fucked me, he told me to look in the mirror and to look at how sexy my body was. He went on to describe how perfect my tits and curves were. I started to get turned on not only by his words, but by the process of appreciating my own body. I did look hot with him fucking me.

I spent the next two weeks rigorously working on my book. I edited, had my friends read it and give me feedback, then edited it some more. All in all, the reviews were great. I was sad that Chase was busy and didn't have time to read my story, but luckily my friends and mom were able to give me feedback. On Friday afternoon, I was ready to send the finished story off to my agent and then play the waiting game to get the publisher's feedback. I was so in love with my story that I was confident the publisher would love it, too.

When I pressed send and my book was officially out of my hands for the time being, I felt a sense of relief and accomplishment. I was ready to go out and celebrate all weekend long. Chase wasn't filming that night so we went out as a real couple. We started with dinner at the incredible NoMI restaurant and then met up with his friends and my friends at the famous Chicago nightclub, The Underground, for a real celebration. Vodka was flowing and everyone was having a good time.

On Saturday night, Chase and I stayed in to nurse our hangovers. We ordered in food, took a bath, and gave each other massages. I wanted a donut to help cure my hangover, but Chase didn't like me eating them. He was convinced I had a donut addiction and soon they'd all go to my ass. He used to be in the fitness industry so he was probably right about them. I tried not to eat donuts anymore, at least not when I was at Chase's house.

I was glad to be staying in and resting up because the next day we were headed to a family party where I would be meeting Chase's family for the first time. I had always been curious about his family and wondered what kind of people would create a man who grew up to be a dating and sex expert.

We were up bright and early because we both were asleep by 10 p.m. the night before. We got ready and hit the road to head to the suburbs. We were going to his parent's house so I could meet his parents first and then heading across the street to his aunt and uncle's for his cousin's birthday party. On the drive there, I began to feel nervous. For some reason I was worried that his family might not like me. I think Chase sensed my nervousness and grabbed my hand. I felt little butterflies in my body, which overrode the nervousness. He told me not to worry because his family would love me and continued on with telling me all the things he loved about me. He always made me feel so confident.

We arrived at his parents' home and they were waiting outside for our arrival on the front porch. I took a deep breath and got out of the car. When we walked onto the porch, I was welcomed with hugs and excitement. His parents were so sweet. Chase must've talked me up quite a bit because they seemed to think the world of me. His mother had even bought my first two novels and read them. I was a little surprised because my books were a bit racy and if she read my next book, she might be in for a shock because I was really starting to explore sex more in my writing. His mom said she loved my writing, though, and couldn't wait to read the one she heard I was working on.

I found the common denominator of reading to get to know Chase's mother and talking with his father came even easier. He was a fun-loving guy who just wanted everyone to be happy. The thing I loved most about his parents was that you could see their love. They had been married for well over thirty years, and their love was still so apparent. I could only hope for a life filled with such love.

We headed across the street to the family party and although I knew he came from a big family, I was in for a shock. There were people and kids running around everywhere. It was a lot like my family parties, but I never realized how overwhelming it can be for an outsider. I must've been introduced to sixty people that day, but could only remember three of their names. I realized getting to know Chase's family was going to be a process.

In the middle of the party, Chase grabbed my hand and said he needed to run across the street to get more ice from his parents' house. He asked me to join him. I went because I was scared to be left alone in such madness. On our way across the street to his parents' Chase said to me, "I'm going to fuck you in my parents' basement."

I felt my pussy jump. I wasn't expecting that at all. It was so daring and exciting that I could feel my panties get wet as we walked across the street. When we got inside his parent's house, Chase checked to make sure nobody was there before we snuck downstairs. I was wearing a sundress so all I had to do was drop my moist panties and lift up my dress. Chase dropped his shorts and then pulled me toward him from behind. When he penetrated me I grabbed onto the wall for balance. He fucked me hard and he fucked me fast and although I didn't get off, I was riding the wave of excitement. It was so dangerous knowing that anyone in his family could walk in on us fucking at anytime. If we got caught, I would forever be known as a skank in his family's eyes, but the rush was worth the risk.

We cleaned up, went upstairs and went back to the family party across the street, but we didn't realize that our little sexcapade made us forget the ice. Chase was rocking the after-sex glow and I think his cousin noticed because he said, "Where's the ice?" followed by a secret high-five. I didn't care if his cousin knew we just fucked as long as his parents and grandmother didn't know. I wanted them to like me, even though they had to have an idea that I was really sexual if I was dating their son and grandson, a sex expert.

Chase's mom and I ended the night sitting on the porch with a glass of wine talking about reading and crafts while Chase and his dad got caught up on *Sports Center* inside. It was a beautiful night and I was really enjoying getting to know Chase's mom. I was enjoying hearing stories about Chase as a child even more. He was a troublemaker and an attention seeker since the day he was born, two of the many qualities that drew me to him.

When we pulled into the garage at the Trump that night, before getting out of the car, Chase looked at me and said, "I am even more in love with you today than yesterday. My God you are beautiful and perfect for me."

I smiled at him and gave him a kiss before I said, "I really enjoyed meeting your family today."

Chase responded, "They love you."

I asked, "How do you know?"

"I know they love you because I heard it from my dad, my mom, my sister, my brother, my aunt, my grandma, and so on."

"They are loveable people so they have probably loved all the girls you have brought home."

"I haven't really brought many women home."

I said with skepticism, "Sure you haven't."

Chase shook his head back and forth a little as he said, "No, they met my ex-wife, my ..."

Chase had been married? Why did he never tell me this? I asked, "Your ex-wife?"

He said, "Yes, I was married for a few years," like it was no big deal.

I asked, "When?"

Chase gave a look like he was thinking about his answer for a few seconds before he said, "We got married about eight or nine years ago, divorced six years ago."

"How come you never told me?"

"It was so long ago and I moved on from it to start my new path."

"You must've been young."

"Yeah, we weren't even old enough to drink

alcohol at the restaurant we went to the night I proposed to her."

"Why did you get married so young?"

"She was my high school sweetheart and everyone in my family seems to marry their high school sweetheart. I was young and just thought that was what I was supposed to do."

"This is so crazy to me that you were once married."

"Does it bother you? It shouldn't. It was so long ago."

"No, it doesn't bother me, but I am a little shocked by it. Why did you get divorced?"

"We were no longer serving each other."

"What do you mean by 'serving each other?'"

"We were great for each other in high school and through college, but I had a company to build and she wasn't as supportive about it as I would have liked her to be."

"Any more big secrets I should know about?"

Chase changed the subject and asked, "Want to fuck in the back seat and christen my car before we head upstairs?"

I responded, "I would be delighted."

While I was patiently awaiting a response from my publisher about my book, I spent a lot of time at Chase's condo. He was working on his advanced sex life seminar, so it was a great time to be at his place. I would be his dummy for two days as he would explore new ways to pleasure a woman. Life truly didn't get any better than this. He began gently with eating my pussy for what seemed liked hours. How his tongue kept going for so long is beyond me. He pretty much pitched a tent down by my pussy and just tried new little moves. All I had to do was give him positive or negative feedback as he went along. Until now, I didn't realize how many pleasurable buttons the pussy has. His tongue worked my pussy like magic for hours and he looked so sexy doing it.

After I had reached three orgasms, I requested a break. My body and pussy were overwhelmed with pleasure. He let me have a little break and we went for a walk in the park. As we walked, he reviewed the plays he made on my pussy and determined which would be best to teach the men attending his seminar. We stopped for dinner on our way home and then Chase was back to attacking my body with pleasure. He had me lie down on the bed and relax. He lit candles and put on spa-like music.

Once I was fully relaxed, he applied pressure to specific trigger points on my body. He was searching for places men could put pressure on to increase a woman's orgasm. In the process he told me that he was working on developing a trigger point on me by pressing on the top of my left shoulder when I orgasmed sometimes. I never even noticed him doing it. He said it would eventually turn into a button and he could press it and make me orgasm at any time when we were fucking. I had no idea that this was something that could be done.

After pressure-point searching, Chase said he couldn't take it anymore and he had to put his cock inside of me. He penetrated me slowly and seemed to poke around my pussy with his cock searching for my various G-spots. It was nice having him just there inside of me, using his cock to discover me. He used the head of his cock to tease the inside top of my pussy and then would dive deep and push on spots that I didn't even know existed so deep inside of me. After at least a half-hour of his cock discovering my pussy, he began to speed up his penetration. It sent shivers through my body knowing that I was no longer going to be teased with pleasure slowly, but that he was ready to make me orgasm. He held my legs far apart and fucked me deep until I came. He finished right after me, blowing his load all over my stomach.

He lay down next to me and said, "Class resumes tomorrow morning."

I let out a laugh, but he was serious. I woke up in the morning to him massaging my asshole. It sounds like it would be a rude awakening, but it was actually quite pleasurable. He massaged it slowly and softly and since I was asleep, I was already relaxed. He whispered to me, "I can't wait for the day when you let me fuck you in the ass."

That was one thing about me; as much as I love sex and exploring new things, I hadn't reached the point where I was ready to try anal sex. So many women had told me how wonderful it was, but even more women had told me how horrible it was. I was getting closer to wanting to try it, but now I was intimidated because of the size of Chase's cock. I lay there enjoying the anal massage and after a little while he penetrated my pussy with his cock, but continued to massage my anus. He moved in and out of my pussy slowly and it felt pleasurably calming. I could lay there for hours with him doing this. Soon he moved from massaging the outside of my anus to pushing his finger inside slowly. He moved it in and out of my asshole while his cock penetrated my pussy. It felt truly amazing. Gradually, he increased the speed of moving his cock in and out of my pussy and I felt my pussy and asshole tightening up with pleasure. I never realized that the light touch of an asshole while being penetrated with a cock in the pussy could cause so much pleasure. He stopped moving his finger in and out of my asshole, but kept it inside while he fucked my pussy faster and faster until I came. Before my orgasm even finished, I felt him pull his cock out of my pussy and cum all over my ass.

Chase lay down next to me in the bed and asked, "What did you think?"

I said, "Surprisingly, I enjoyed it."

"I just loved feeling your asshole. I really can't wait for the day you let me put my cock in there."

"We'll get there."

As he said, "Oh, I know we will, baby," I saw him move his hand up to rub his eye. I screamed out, "No, don't touch your eye with that hand! You'll get pink eye!"

He pulled his hand away and laughed for a second before he said, "I better go wash my hands."

My pussy got a break because Chase had to go do an appearance on a radio show. I had nothing to do because I hadn't heard from my publisher yet so I joined him. I loved seeing him in action. As he sat with headphones on and a microphone in front of him, he looked so cool, calm, collected, and sexy. Although the radio show host called him and what he does a hoax, Chase handled it like a pro and ended up leaving with the show's host believing in his program. Chase had a magic way of changing people's minds.

On our way home from the show, we stopped to meet one of his clients he was coaching for lunch. This was the first time I got to sit in on a coaching meeting. I had heard him hundreds of times on the phone coaching his clients because some called all hours of the night, but I had never seen him in action face to face. The client that we met was in a relationship, but having issues because the romance had died. Chase told him exactly what steps he needed to start taking to re-establish their relationship. It was almost like Chase was a relationship superhero: saving love lives one relationship at a time.

After the meeting it was time to resume our personal sex class and I couldn't wait to see what Chase had in store for pleasuring me. On the way home we stopped at a sex store where he picked up a few vibrating toys. When we got home, Chase instructed me to undress completely and lay down on the bed. He washed off the toys while I undressed and then joined me in the bedroom. When he came in he put all the toys on the bed and told me to pick one and pleasure myself. I asked, "By myself?"

He responded, "Yes, I want to watch you."

I had briefly masturbated in front of men before, but I never had a guy stand at the end of the bed with his hand on his chin observing every last move I made to pleasure myself. I was a little nervous and wished I had ordered a second glass of wine at lunch. I did as he asked, though, and chose the pink vibrator to start. I turned it on low and slowly moved it around my labia. I looked up at Chase and he was watching me intensely. He said, "Pretend I'm not even here, baby."

I said, "Can you at least take your shirt off?"

He agreed and took his shirt off, but he quickly got back to looking at me with strong observation. Chase looked so fucking hot with his shirt off, but I was still distracted knowing he was watching my every move. I decided to close my eyes and envision him down there, eating my pussy. The thought of his tongue running up and down my labia got me wet fast. I continued to run the vibrator up and down my labia, but pulled it away for a few minutes to massage my pussy with my fingers. As I moved around, I could feel the cum spreading out around my labia. I slowly moved my fingers in and out of my pussy and I could feel them getting sticky with cum. I moved my fingers up to my mouth and tasted myself. I tasted good. I grabbed the vibrator again and placed it directly on my clit. I applied full pressure and increased the speed until I felt my pussy tighten and body pulsate with pleasure. When I opened my eyes, Chase was taking his pants off. He said, "That is one of the hottest fucking things I have ever seen. I need to fuck you right now."

He jumped onto the bed and penetrated me. I was still coming down from my orgasm high, but I could feel my cum gathering on his cock and dripping out of my pussy. He fucked me fast and came before I had even come completely down from my orgasm. He lay next to me and I said, "I think I need to take a break for the rest of the day. My pussy is getting sore!"

Chase agreed that he, too, was getting sore and that he was okay with taking the rest of the day off. He said he had explored enough to start working on his advanced sex life seminar. We cuddled for a little bit while we listened to a recording of the radio show he was on earlier in the day. After that, I headed home. I hadn't been home in quite a few days and Nikki was getting impatient with me ignoring her so I invited her over for a wine and movie night.

I finally heard back from my publisher that they liked my book, but they found some parts to be too foul. They sent me edits on what they wanted me to change. I spent hours and hours going over the areas they wanted me to change, but couldn't get myself to agree to any of the changes they wanted. I felt like it was compromising my writing. I talked to my agent and explained my concern. My agent came back telling me that the publisher would not publish my book without these changes. I went back and forth because I wanted my story to be read, but in my gut I felt that the intense sexual descriptions were needed and if taken out, they would compromise the story. I asked my agent if she could find me a new publisher, explaining that if they weren't willing to publish this story as is, they wouldn't be interested in my future writings in which I planned to go even deeper with the sexual descriptions. She didn't recommend moving publishers and had to review my contract, but agreed to see what she could do.

A couple of days later, she got back to me and said she would start shopping around for a new publisher. I was back to the waiting game, but had agreed to start writing for Chase's company's website so that kept me busy along with plenty of new articles for the *RedEye*.

Chase himself kept me the busiest. He wanted me around all the time and I was staying at his place more than my own. I was practically living there and had filled up all the open space he made for me with my stuff.

Since I was there so much, I felt like even though the sex was still amazing, I wanted to do something different. We always drove past this really old motel that had hourly rates. It looked ghetto and we joked that someday we'd fuck at that motel or a motel that had hourly rates. While Chase was out at several coaching meetings, I took the "L" train up north to pick out some new and risky stuff to play with while we fucked. The best sex shops in Chicago are located in Boys Town and when I walked in the first one, I felt like a kid in a candy store. It was a slow afternoon and I was the only one in the store so Steven, a super eccentric and sexually advanced gay guy, helped me shop. I told Steven about my plan to surprise Chase at the old motel and he thought it was a superb idea. He was such a delight and taught me so many new ways to pleasure a cock. I really should get more advice from gay men about pleasuring a cock. They had to be so knowledgeable because they got it from both ends; they gave and they received pleasure with a cock.

Steven picked out a whole smorgasbord of corset lingerie sets for me to try on. With each one that I tried on, I felt more and more sexually powerful. He brought me thigh high fishnet stockings and six-inch heel boots to go with the dangerous ensemble I picked out. After I decided on the ensemble, Steven and I moved on to picking out a leather whip. Just holding it in my hand sent a charge through my body. Steven recommended a ball strap to go on Chase, which could intensify his orgasm. *How could I not buy something that would make his orgasm more intense?* I also bought a gag ball, straps to tie Chase up, and a new fancy blindfold. I figured this was enough for today. As I was checking out, Steven threw in a bunch of samples of lubricants, massage oils, and soaps. When I was walking out the door I spotted a sex swing and I wanted to buy it badly, but decided against it because I didn't want to carry it on the "L" train all the way back to Chase's.

When I got to Chase's condo, I showered up and packed a bag with all my new sex items. I walked over to the hourly rate motel, because it was a nice evening, and I wanted to stop for a donut. I also knew I had time to kill until Chase would be finished with his last coaching meeting. He synced our calendars, so I could keep track of his busy schedule. When I walked up to the motel, I took a picture of the sign before entering to check in. Inside, it smelled like stale cigarettes and mothballs, which oddly reminded me of when I went to my great grandfather's house as a kid. I checked in requesting five hours, which was only $60. If we wanted to stay longer we could, they would just charge me when I checked out. I got the key, which was an actual key and not a key card. I was feeling like I had taken a trip back in time.

Once in the trashy motel room, I sent a text to Chase with the photo of the motel's sign that said, "Room 115. Don't keep me waiting."

I started to get dressed in my new bondage-style corset ensemble when Chase texted me back, "For real?"

I simply replied, "Yes."

A few minutes passed and I figured Chase was working on getting out of whatever it was he was doing so he could get to me as soon as possible, but then my phone rang and I knew it was him by the ringtone. I answered, "Are you on your way? I want your cock in my mouth!"

"What the fuck is this?"

"It's a surprise."

"I HATE surprises. You know that."

"It's not like it is a party with a bunch of people, I just want you to meet me here to put your cock in my mouth."

"What am I supposed to do with the plans I made for tonight?"

"I didn't know you had plans. Your calendar was open."

"Well, I made plans to go to an event. I am so pissed right now. What do you expect me to do?"

"Alright, alright, we can do this at another time."

"You know full well that if I could plan out every second of every day I would. I like to be prepared for things."

"I was just trying to be spontaneous and do something nice and fun for you."

"Oh really, you are doing this for me? If you were doing this for me, then you wouldn't fucking surprise me."

"I'm sorry this upsets you. I just wanted to do something nice."

"Next time you do something nice take into

consideration what that person likes and dislikes and if it's me remember that I absolutely fucking hate surprises!"

"Duly noted."

"So do I just cancel with these guys so I can come fuck you or do I disappoint you and not meet you? Either way, I am going to let down someone."

"I won't be disappointed. We can do it another time or even later tonight."

"So what are you just going to sit at that trashy motel until I am finished with these guys?"

"I can do that."

"No, I don't want you sitting there for hours waiting on me."

"I'll be fine. I can download a book on my phone and read or the sign out front said they have HBO."

"Audrey, listen to my words very carefully: never surprise me with anything again. Am I making myself clear?"

"Crystal clear, Chase. I am going to head home. You enjoy the night with the guys and I will make a plan for us to do this another time."

"You really just ruined my night making me seem like the asshole who disappointed you."

"You didn't disappoint me. I understand. Now go enjoy your night."

After I hung up the phone, all I could think was what the fuck? What was his problem? Did he seriously have that much of an issue with surprises? I was annoyed and had no desire to see him so I went back to his place, got my computer, and headed back to my apartment. I hadn't been home in a week so a night away from him was probably good anyway. On my way home, I called Nikki and we met up for a few drinks at the local watering hole between our apartments. I needed food, too, since I hadn't gotten groceries at my place in weeks. Vodka helped clear my confusion. I was home and in bed by 10:30 p.m. Even though Chase's bed was much more luxurious than mine and I preferred sleeping with him next to me, it felt nice to be in my own bed and alone. I snuggled in and fell fast asleep.

I wasn't asleep very long when I heard pounding on my door. I walked out of my room and to my door. When I opened it, I saw Chase on the other side crying. He wept out, "Why weren't you home when I got there and why haven't you been answering my calls? I'm so sorry I disappointed you. Please don't leave me!"

Chase needed to settle the fuck down. I wasn't leaving him over this. I was just giving us a little space for the night. I tried to be nice and I pulled him into my apartment and led him over to my couch. I wrapped my arms around him and said, "I'm not going anywhere. You didn't disappoint me. I just thought a night apart might be good. You were pretty heated earlier."

"I got so scared when I got home and you weren't there. I thought you left me."

"It's just a night."

"Why didn't you call me or text me and tell me you were leaving?"

"You are right and I should've let you know. I will be better at communicating."

"Please don't abandon me, please."

"Oh honey, I am not going anywhere, don't you worry."

I wiped the tears off his face and kissed him. He wept a little more in my arms and he asked if he could sleep here with me tonight. We went into my room and crawled into bed. No foreplay and no sex, we lay there as I rubbed his back until he fell asleep. As I rubbed his back and watched his cute face sleep, I wondered why he had been so upset about the motel surprise and why he was acting so insecure. Had I done something to make him feel this way? I was even more confused now.

I woke up in the morning to Chase kissing the back of my neck. I opened my eyes and turned over to look at him and he said, "Promise you will never leave me. I love you and I need you."

I said, "I'm not going anywhere," and then kissed him. The kiss slowly led into us making love. We didn't fuck, we made love. It was slow and it was emotional. I felt a connection to him that I had never felt before and it scared me a little. I knew I had fallen in love with him, but at this moment, I was feeling something that almost seemed like it was more. It was a bit overwhelming and I think Chase felt it, too, because he began crying saying, "I just love you so much, baby."

All of these emotions and feelings had me confused. I didn't know what was going on and for some reason, I started to feel like crying, too. I felt all weird and emotional inside and I didn't know how to stop it. Maybe I was getting my period? All of a sudden, I burst into tears and said, "I love you so much."

Now we were both crying and his dick was losing girth by the second. He pulled his cock out of my pussy and pulled me into his arms. He held me tight as we both lay there crying like a bunch of ninnies. It was completely ridiculous. After several minutes of crying, I started to laugh and said, "What is wrong with us?"

Chase began to laugh too and said, "We just have so much love."

"But why the fuck are we crying so much?"

"We are connecting on a new level."

"Well, connect your cock with my pussy and let's fuck. No more crying."

I put my hand on his cock and stroked it until it was hard enough to push inside of my pussy. He inserted it slowly and gradually increased the speed. I kept thinking about crying for reasons unknown, but tried to get it out of my head so I could enjoy the sex. It was hard to block out, but I managed to push it aside in my brain enough to allow me to reach a weak orgasm. It was one of those orgasms that you have and you get pissed because it wasn't worth all the effort you had to put in to reach it. I prayed that this kind of situation was just a fluke.

Chase left to go home before he had to speak at a seminar. I stayed home, but assured him I would be back at his place that evening. I didn't want him freaking out and crying that I was abandoning him again, causing me to cry for no fucking reason. On the outside, Chase projected himself as so confident and secure, but lately I had been noticing that he was not as confident and secure as I thought.

I ran a bath and called Nikki to see if she ever cried like that during sex. As I was explaining what had gone down with Chase, I hopped into the bathtub. As I soaked in the bathtub, I went on and on telling Nikki the motel story. As I was talking I looked down and noticed, there was a hair on my nipple. It was really short, but thick and black so I thought that it was a miscellaneous hair that had fallen off Chase's chest onto me. I went to pull it off and realized it was connected to me; it was hair from my body on my nipple! I said to Nikki, "Dude, there's a hair on my nipple."

She responded, "Tweeze it out, idiot."

I asked, "Why am I growing a hair on my nipple?"

"Shit, dude, I get nipple hairs all the time. Just tweeze it."

"This is normal?"

"I've been getting random hairs on my nipples for at least five years. Consider yourself lucky it is just starting now."

"Just starting?"

"Just wait, there will be more."

Oh great, now I had to deal with nipple hairs? This was not my day. It started with crying sex, then there was a dud of an orgasm, now I had a hair on my nipple. I hoped Chase never saw or felt the nipple hair. What if he had? No, he would've said something if he had. I think. How fucking embarrassing!

DATING CHASE WALKER

Since Chase and I reached a point where we were apparently so emotionally connected that I couldn't even understand it, I figured it was time for him to meet my family. I had been avoiding it because I was still unsure how I was going to look my father in the eyes and tell him I was dating a sex expert. Plus, I don't know why, but I had this odd feeling that my mother wouldn't like him. My family is a little out there and would probably think it's cool as shit, but I still worried. Mostly I worried that their hippy lifestyle would scare Chase off.

My parents are interesting characters. My father is an environmental lawyer and my mother is a librarian. Growing up, we recycled, ate organic and composted before it was cool. Friends never wanted to come to my house because snacks consisted of nuts and fruits instead of Twinkies and potato chips, but when we were in high school and everyone realized my father was a stoner that changed. My dad left his weed out in his workshop and had quite the stash. I didn't smoke weed, but many of my friends did and I let them steal some here and there.

On our drive out for a weekend at my parent's lake house, I briefed Chase on my family. He didn't seem nervous at all. He said he knew how to win people over, especially parents. Along with my parents, my grandma and a bunch of my aunts, uncles and cousins would be there. It was only one night, but my family could be pretty overwhelming.

When we pulled up to the lake house, my parents weren't standing out front waiting for us like his parents were when I first met them. Instead, we walked into the house and people were running around screaming at one another. My cousins were running around chasing one another with swords, my uncle was sitting on the couch yelling at my cousins to stop running around and my aunt was yelling at my uncle to control his children. I introduced Chase to my aunt, uncle and cousins and then we went out to the backyard where everyone was hanging out. Everyone shut up and looked at us when we walked outside. I said, "Hi everyone, this is Chase."

In unison they all said, "Hi, Chase."

I pointed to each person saying their name and Chase waved to them after I said who they were. I asked my mom what bedroom Chase and I were going to sleep in and she said that the inn was full so we would be on a blow-up mattress in the living room. I brought my mother to the side and said, "Mom, I don't think Chase will be comfortable with that."

My mom responded, "That's too bad. You guys are only here one night. You'll be fine."

I told Chase we were stuck on a blow-up mattress in the living room and he said he came from a big family and understood. He then leaned in and whispered in my ear, "I'm still going to find a way to fuck you while we are here because we need to add some new stuff to our sex journal."

I said, "I already have a plan."

At some point over the weekend, I wanted to get Chase in the shed to fuck. It would be tight and it would be hot as fuck, but that's what made it sound fun to me. I agreed with Chase and we hadn't been as adventurous with sex lately. We needed something scandalous, trashy, and new.

Chase and I went inside and got our swimsuits out of our bags before heading upstairs to change. Since everyone was outside, I pulled Chase into the bathroom with me and told him to fuck me hard and fast. His dick rose to attention right away and he put it inside of me. I stood holding onto the sink for balance while he fucked me from behind. It was hard and fast like I requested and after just a couple of minutes, he pulled out and came in the sink. I ran the water to wash the cum down the drain and then put on my bathing suit. We walked downstairs, stopping in the kitchen for a cocktail. My father bought a new margarita machine so we thought we'd try one. With our margaritas, we walked outside and joined the family.

I really wanted Chase to get to know my grandma. She and I had always been really close and I am pretty sure I got my pervertedness from her. My grandma didn't say much, but when she did, it was always quick-witted and slightly uncomfortable to hear coming out of an old lady's mouth. The only advice she ever gave me was to find a man that I couldn't keep my hands off of and who couldn't keep his hands off of me. She said relationships weren't just about sex, but that sex and passion for one another could get you through any hard time. If my granny was right, then Chase was the man for me.

Chase and I sat down next to my grandma and she instructed me to go get her another Pabst Blue Ribbon beer from the refrigerator. For a moment I worried about what she would say to Chase while I was gone, but I knew he was confident enough to handle anything. After retrieving my grandma's beer, I walked back outside and saw my grandma whispering in Chase's ear. I wondered what she was saying to him. I approached them and she pulled away from him smiling. I asked, "Are you guys talking about me?"

My grandma responded, "Mind your business," and they both laughed. I sat down and tried to convince them to tell me about their secret, but neither my grandma nor Chase would budge on letting the cat out of the bag. I decided to let it go.

As we sat by the lake that afternoon, I admired Chase and his ability to take anything that came to him. My family wasn't always easy to handle and they loved making the "new guy" feel uncomfortable. My uncle asked Chase what he did for a living and Chase began explaining exactly what a dating and sex expert did. My uncle was completely blown away by what Chase did so in the middle of Chase telling him, he insisted everyone gather around Chase and listen. As people joined into the conversation, I could tell they were shocked by what he did. And when Chase told them about the sex seminars he taught, everyone looked at me for confirmation that he actually did know what he was talking about. As open and odd as my family was, I had never felt this uncomfortable around them before.

As glad as I was to have the cat out of the bag and Chase there to explain what he did for a living, I still felt like everyone there was looking at me funny. I decided to excuse myself and go inside for a margarita refill. I hung out inside for a few minutes and when my father came in to refill his drink, I couldn't look him in the eye. He was insistent on talking to me, though, and said, "That's quite a catch you got out there."

I was surprised those were the words he chose to speak and not something along the lines of how did I raise such a whore? I simply said, "He's great, Dad. I really like this one."

He responded with a smile saying, "I know you do; I can see it in your eyes."

I slightly questioned him asking, "Really?"

"Absolutely. And don't be ashamed of what he does. He's very passionate about it. I know I've never read your novels, but that's only because I like to pretend you don't write those dirty things. I know that you love writing and if that's what makes you happy, I support it and would never deny what you do to another. You shouldn't deny him his passion."

My father was right. Chase's passion was actually part of the reason I fell for him. I said, "I know and I usually don't. I am just scared of the family judging me."

"This family? Shit, this family judges everyone for everything, but they love you just the same."

The talk with my father actually made me feel better. If I was going to be with Chase, I had to support and love what he did no matter what. Even though what Chase did for a living was taboo, he was happy and I was happy being with him. I wasn't ashamed that I wrote about sex so why should I be ashamed that he taught it?

After the family drilled Chase with questions for a good hour, I pulled him away to take a ride on the paddleboat with me. It was my attempt to give him serenity for a little while. We paddled out to the middle of the lake. When we got out there, I apologized for the interrogation made by my family. He said he enjoyed it. He was of a different breed. I would've been panicking if his family interrogated me that way. He said, "I love the rush I get proving myself to those who doubt me."

I asked, "Doesn't it bother you that they doubt you?"

"Not for a second. Now, am I allowed to finger you out here on this paddle boat?"

"I don't know if you are allowed to, but I am all for breaking rules."

Chase leaned in giving me a long passionate kiss while he slowly moved my bathing suit bottom to the side and began to finger me. I loved feeling any piece of him inside of me. As he moved his index and middle finger in and out of my pussy, he slowly massaged my clit with his thumb. I so badly wanted to take my bikini bottom off and open my legs wide, but my family was only a few hundred feet behind us.

He continued fingering me discreetly and when I looked down I could see my cum all over his fingers. I looked his sexy body up and down and he looked back at me smiling while biting his lip. That's when I couldn't control myself and I felt my body tense up before it released a small, but pleasurable orgasm.

After I came, he kissed me and we got back to paddling around the lake. We held hands and we didn't say much, we'd look at each other here and there and our looks would say a thousand words. It was there, out on the lake, that I knew I didn't want to spend another day without this man in my life. There was just something about him that made me feel more alive than I had ever felt in my life.

I heard back from my agent and she found a publisher that loved my novel. They wanted to publish it and requested I tweak the ending just a tiny bit so we could turn it into a series. Originally, I didn't want any changes made to my book, but I considered tweaking it a little bit. Writing a book series would be fun. I loved the story line and felt I could take the characters even further. I sat down and brainstormed for a few days on where I could take the storyline and the characters to make it into a series. Chase was extremely busy so I had days to myself. I outlined my series' ideas and sent them to my agent. The next day I was on a conference call with the publisher. They thought my ideas were fantastic and encouraged me to push my limits when writing the sexual scenarios within the book.

I was glad I followed my gut and didn't compromise my writing by publishing with my old publisher. Not only was the new publisher going to be paying me $10,000 more and 2% more on royalties, but they were also pushing me to do a series. I got to work tweaking my original ending right away and even started the first two chapters of the second book in the series. I felt like I was on a high and glad Chase was so busy with his work. It gave me the time I needed to get the ball rolling. I had my period anyway so it felt good to be home.

But, after three nights away from Chase, I started missing him. My period ended so I texted him asking what time I could come over. He said he had a full afternoon and had to judge a fashion show that night, but should be home by eleven. I told him I'd be at his place by the time he got home and he said hearing that made his day. A few minutes later, he texted me saying, "I'm so fucking horny."

I was, too. He had no idea. The first few days after my period ends, I am at my horniest. I responded, "So am I!" with a winking face.

I met Bree for dinner and then headed to Chase's. He wasn't home yet so I poured myself a glass of wine and worked on the second book for my series. A little before eleven, Chase sent me a text that said he was running late and wouldn't be home for at least another hour. I had hit a roadblock with writing so I refilled my glass of wine and took a bath in his big Jacuzzi bathtub. The relaxation of my bath made me tired, but I wanted to stay up and get laid. I crawled onto his bed, searched through Netflix and put on one of my all-time favorite movies, *An Affair to Remember*. As much as I couldn't wait to get to the emotional Empire State Building scene where two lovers are to finally meet again, I was just too exhausted and fell asleep.

As I was sleeping, I felt Chase crawl into bed with me. He was quiet and didn't even attempt to wake me up for sex. He just crawled in, snuggled me and was snoring quickly after. I was still half asleep so I thought "Screw it" to waking up for sex. I'm sure I'd wake up to his hard dick poking my back in the morning, anyway.

In the middle of the night, I woke up again because Chase was fidgeting in his sleep. He was making moaning noises that sounded as if he were in pain. I thought he might be having a bad dream so I moved closer to him to cuddle him and let him know I was here for him. As I went to cuddle him, he felt hot, much hotter than the normal amount of heat he expelled when he slept. I put my hands on his body and he was burning up. I then put my hand on his forehead to confirm that he was really burning up. I said, "Chase" in attempt to wake him up. He needed to take some fever reducer or something. He didn't wake up, though, so I said his name again. When he opened his eyes I told him he was burning up. He asked me to go get the painkillers out of the kitchen and some water. I did as he asked and when I came back, he asked me to go into his closet and open the humidor. He said in it was a bowl and some weed. I went and got the bowl and weed as instructed and handed it to him. I asked, "Where's your thermometer?"

He responded, "Top middle drawer in the bathroom. In the back."

I got the thermometer and held it in his mouth while he packed the bowl with weed. I said, "Maybe you caught the flu or something?"

He said with agitation, "No, it's my fever disease."

I asked, "Your fever disease?"

"The generic name for it is Periodic Fever Syndrome."

"How long have you had this?"

"My whole life."

The thermometer beeped and I took it out of his mouth. I said, "Shit, your temperature is 104.3. I've never known someone to have a fever so high."

As he was exhaling the drag he had taken of weed he said, "It's not the worst fever I've had."

I asked, "Should we go to the hospital?"

"No, it could come down at any time. Sometimes it stays for a few hours and other times a week." He took a few more hits off his bowl and then said, "Just hold me. Just tell me I am going to be okay. Just tell me you love me."

I had no idea what to expect, but I did as he asked. He was so fucking hot that I started sweating and took my shirt off. I pressed my boobs up to his back and held him tight, telling him over and over again that I was here for him. He was quiet and I can only assume he was in a daze from all the weed he had smoked. After a little while I felt him fall asleep. I couldn't sleep, though. I was scared and I didn't know what to expect. I also wondered why he hadn't told me about this disease before. He fidgeted in his sleep and I held him tight. I wasn't sure what else I could do except lie there and keep an eye on him.

After an hour or so, he woke up weeping from the pain. I was surprised because by now the painkillers should've taken control of his body. He cried out, "Hold me and tell me everything is going to be okay."

I hated seeing him in pain, but all I could do was be there for him. He asked for more drugs and I gave them to him. I suggested a cool bath to bring down the fever and he said okay. I ran the bath and then called him into the bathroom when the tub was full. I watched him as he slowly dipped himself into the cool water. He looked so uncomfortable, but sat down. Once he was sitting in the water, he began to weep some more while screaming out how painful it was. I wished I could do more for him. I brought him his bowl of weed and he smoked it while sitting in the bathtub. After several minutes in there, he said he couldn't take it anymore and wanted to go back in the bed. I helped him out of the tub and followed him to the bed. He lay down fully naked on the bed. His body was still wet, but I think the cool air on his body was good for him. I lay down next to him and gently ran my fingers up and down his body while he wept some more in pain. When he fell asleep, I just watched him. Seeing him like this made me love him even more. I thought to myself that I would do anything, even take the pain on myself, to make him feel better.

I kept rubbing his arm until I became so tired I could no longer keep my eyes open. I slept for a little while, but not fully. I was half asleep and half awake to make sure I was available if he needed me. After a few hours, he began fidgeting and weeping in his sleep again. I woke Chase and handed him a couple more painkillers to take along with his bowl of weed. He took the pills and a few hits and went back to sleep.

Late that morning, I felt the sun hitting my face from a small crack in the drapes. Chase still felt really hot. I wanted to wake him up to take his temperature again, but he looked like he was peacefully sleeping. I laid there waiting for over an hour until I saw him fidgeting again. I woke him up and put the thermometer in his mouth. His fever had gone down a little bit, but it was still showing 103.1. He took some more painkillers and hits of weed and went back to sleep. I grabbed my laptop and sat next to him in bed writing and ready in case he needed me.

About an hour passed before he woke up and yelled out, "I'm going to throw-up!"

I hated vomit. I am the type of person that gags and sometimes throws up when I see someone else throw up, but I told myself to be strong for Chase. I rushed with him into the bathroom where he squatted down next to the toilet and vomited. I rubbed his back, but then stepped away to grab a wet washcloth to wipe his face with. As I was running cool water on the washcloth, I looked at him as he was squatting next to the toilet. He looked so vulnerable. I also noticed that his limp dick was hanging low between his legs and almost touching the ground. I told myself to snap out of it and that right now was not a time to be thinking about his cock.

After vomiting several times, I wiped his face off before he went back to lie in bed. It was apparent the painkillers were upsetting his stomach. I was proud of myself for not gagging once while he vomited. I got him a Gatorade to drink and heated up a can of chicken noodle soup. He drank the Gatorade, but refused the soup even though I insisted he eat a little bit. I lightly rubbed his back until he fell asleep. Once he was asleep, I got back to writing and browsing Facebook to kill the time.

I sat in the bed next to him the entire day just writing and browsing the web, only stopping when Chase woke up and needed me. Chase had me text his assistant Mary just the word, "fever." Apparently, when he got sick like this, she would cancel all meetings for the day. She understood the code word and didn't ask any questions.

By midnight his fever was down to 102, but he was still uncomfortable. I kept giving him weed to make him feel a little less pain. By sunrise the next day, his fever had almost disappeared. I continued to give him his painkillers and weed until he told me to stop. A fever that high and intense can fuck with your mind and body and I wasn't sure how long the recovery process was.

I sent another text message to Mary with the code word "fever." Even if Chase insisted on working today I wasn't going to let him. When I was browsing the Internet, I looked up his condition. I couldn't find that much information on it, but from what I did find, it looked like this was a very serious disease and needed to be monitored from start through recovery. Some people on discussion boards suggested stress and lack of sleep were triggers. Chase had so much stress with work right now that it could be what triggered this episode. The websites said this disease varied depending on the person. I wished Chase had told me about his illness and prepared me for it. I truly felt useless and just wanted to help.

After another day of sleep and drugs for Chase, his fever was finally gone. He struggled though as he said he felt like a truck had hit him. He stayed home and worked that day taking coaching calls over the phone and responding to hundreds of emails. He was rather lethargic and seemed depressed so I did what I could to cheer him up. Sex was usually my go-to move to help cheer up a man, but he still seemed weak. We did fuck once, briefly, but besides that all I could think of to do was to be there, cook for him, cuddle him, and rub his back. He assured me many times that was more than enough and that soon he'd be back to normal. I wanted him to feel better and back to normal, but there was part of me that felt good that I was able to be there for him in a time of need. Going through this and seeing his vulnerability made me fall more in love with him and as happy as that made me, it scared me, too.

With the crying sex, meeting of the families and Chase's fever episode, our relationship was reaching a new level and our sex was getting a little less adventurous. I decided it was time to put the lingerie, whip, gag ball, and other items I had bought for the motel to use. To avoid any sort of surprise, I told Chase I wanted to plan an adventurous sex night and asked him to put it on his calendar for Thursday night. He agreed.

As I waited for Chase to come home Thursday night, I got his place ready for our sex adventure. I lit candles and placed them throughout his living area and bedroom and picked a sexy Pandora station to play while we got down and dirty. It took me a little while to get dressed up because tying a corset up isn't easy, but I was all dressed and ready before Chase even texted me to let me know he was on his way home. To fill the time while I waited, I drank a glass of wine and it calmed my nervous excitement a little bit. Just wearing my new sexy outfit made me feel powerful and I wanted to be able to act powerful over Chase when he got home. I wanted to take control of him and his body.

I fiddled with the whip a little bit trying it out on my thigh before I went to double check that I had all the items out and ready for use in the bedroom. I took a long look at the ball strap, gag ball, blindfold, and ties while I thought about all the stuff I wanted to happen when using them. While I was in a bit of a trance with my fantasies, I heard my phone beep. Chase texted me saying he was on his way and should be home in ten minutes.

I impatiently waited for him to come in the door by standing by it holding my new whip. When Chase walked into his condo, his eyes widened at the sight of me. He said, "Holy shit! You look fucking hot, baby."

I felt hot. The outfit I was wearing made me feel so sexy and the whip I was holding made me feel in control. Chase gave me a big kiss and told me how he loved coming home to me. I liked him coming home to me, too. I still got butterflies when he would walk into a room. He asked if he could go freshen up before we started and I told him he could if he was quick. I slapped him on the ass with the whip as he walked toward the bedroom.

I sipped on my wine and fiddled with the whip some more until Chase came back wearing only a towel wrapped around his waist. My God, did he look sexy. I was turned on instantly and part of me just wanted to say *fuck all these toys* and have him penetrate me right then and there, but I got my hormones under control. I handed Chase a glass of wine and he took a few sips before asking what I had in store. I said, "Follow me to the bedroom."

In the bedroom, I instructed him to drop his towel and stand completely naked next to the wall. I tied his hands together and kissed him passionately before putting the gag ball in his mouth. I pulled the blindfold over his eyes and moved down to attach the ball strap to his balls. I felt so in control and it was such a turn on. I could feel the cum seeping out of my pussy.

I started out by running the whip gently around his body, but quickly moved into more of an aggressive mode. I directed him to stand to the side and make his dick hard. It had weight to it, but it wasn't fully erect. I slapped him in the ass with the whip and screamed, "Make your cock get hard!" I saw it increase in size just a little bit. I whipped him on the ass again and screamed, "I said make your cock hard!" This time, it made a jump in size, but I kept at it saying, "Harder!" while I slapped him again. I repeated this four more times before having him turn to me.

I got down on my knees and put my mouth on his cock. I could hear him moan in pleasure through the gag ball. I sucked on his cock hard, with the most suction I had ever used. Every once in awhile I'd stop and use a degrading word telling his cock that it wasn't good enough for me. I was being mean to his cock, which had only done nice things for me in the past, but it was ridiculously hard so I was sure it was enjoying itself.

I dropped my panties and led Chase over to the bed. I had him lay down face up and I sat down letting his cock penetrate my pussy. I moved up and down slowly feeling my cum gather around his cock with each movement. As I looked at him, I realized the gag ball was too much. I removed it because I wanted to hear him use words to turn me on. I told him to tell me that I was too good for him and to tell me how lucky he was to have me riding his cock. He pleaded out, "I am not worthy of your pussy. You are too good for me, but please don't stop riding my cock."

I responded, "I'll decide when I will stop riding your cock," and then I smacked him across the face. I felt really bad; I didn't like smacking him around. I did like being in charge, but this was going too far. Chase pleading like a little ninny was actually a bit of a turn off. I decided to free him of his ties and take off the blindfold. I pulled his arm leading him off the bed. I bent over the side of the bed with my legs spread open. I told him to lick my pussy and make me wet. As soon as I felt myself getting turned on again, I told him to penetrate me from behind, grab my hips tight, and fuck me hard. He fucked me deep and hard until I came and then he pulled out and came in my ass crack. I could feel the cum running down and dripping onto the floor.

After Chase wiped the cum out of my ass crack with a washcloth, we lay down on the bed and I said, "I'm sorry."

He asked, "Why?"

"It was just too much for me. I didn't like being mean to you like that."

"Oh, baby, don't you worry. I didn't take any of it personally."

"I know, but it actually started to turn me off. I don't think I am cut out for that type of fucking."

"Be proud of yourself. You took initiative and tried something new. It's a different experience so let's ease into it. You still feel cut out to wear outfits like these, right?" Chase let out a little chuckle.

I looked down at my body as I said, "I do looking fucking hot in this."

"You have no idea. Next time you wear this outfit I am refusing to wear a blindfold."

"Got it!"

Chase pulled me in and held me tight as he said, "I love you, baby, and I love how you make me feel so amazing."

I said with a smile, "I love you, too."

After work one night Chase came home and said, "My God you are just so beautiful," before he asked me, "Would you be interested in having a role in the reality show we are pitching?"

I was a bit taken back by his question because when he was filming he always tried to portray himself as single. I asked, "What kind of role?"

Chase responded, "The role of my girlfriend. You'd move in with me and it would be my way of showing that my shit works."

I asked, "What do you mean works?"

"You are hot, you are sexual, you are funny, and you have a foul mouth. There's also the twist that you write erotic romance."

"I thought you wanted people to think you are single?"

"I've been thinking about it lately and maybe our relationship drama could actually add to the show."

"But we don't have any drama."

"Well, we might have to make some drama up and then let me fix it to show that I apply everything I teach while coaching to my own life."

"I'm just confused because I thought you wanted to come off as a playboy?"

"I did because that was my original vision,

but we haven't had much response so maybe it's time we try something different. I think it would be interesting for people to see that I have a sexy and fucking awesome girlfriend who not only supports what I do, but works with me by writing on my website. On top of that, they could see the adventurous sex life we have as a couple."

With concern I asked, "Wait, they'd see us have sex?"

"No, but we'd talk about things we've done or plan to do."

"Hmm ..."

"We've pitched the show to so many people and haven't gotten any bites. I think it needs more of a woman's touch and I'd really like that woman to be you. It could be a great way to promote your writing if it works out."

"True, I could promote my new book series, but I am just not good on camera. I get all nervous and awkward."

"I'll help you get used to it. We'll start small."

"So I'd be living with you?"

"While filming, yes." Chase smiled as he asked, "Are you interested in moving in here officially with me?"

I hesitated as I said, "Err... umm, I haven't thought about it."

Chase smiled at me as he said, "You know I'd love to have you here all the time."

With confusion I asked, "You would?"

"Absolutely, I like coming home with you being here and I love having you in my bed every night."

"Don't you think it's too soon?"

"I always live in the now, baby. Whatever feels good to me or whatever is best for me at the time is what I do and right now having you around makes me feel great."

"Hmm …"

"Let me give you a foot massage while you think about it."

I accepted the foot massage, and Chase went on trying to convince me to move in, saying it would be a lot of fun and that if the show gets picked up I could make some good money. I didn't really need money anymore. I got a big old check for my book and soon it would be on the shelves and royalties would be rolling in. Plus, Chase paid for pretty much everything so I was stashing cash like never before. More money couldn't hurt, though. It might be nice to be responsible and save for the future or some shit.

I slept on the idea of being a part of Chase's reality show pitch. When I woke up in the morning, I crawled under the sheets and put my mouth on his cock. I sucked on it, feeling it get harder by the moment in my mouth. Once Chase was awake he lifted the sheets up and smiled at me. I took my mouth off his cock and used it as a microphone as I told him I'd give this reality show thing a try. He pulled me up and kissed me with excitement. He said, "This is going to be so much fun!" before flipping me on my back and penetrating me. He fucked me with a smile on his face, which made me smile, too.

After we both orgasmed, we lay in bed naked, catching our breath and throwing around ideas on what to film for the show. I couldn't believe that I might be on a reality TV show. This was completely out of my character, but the rush of going beyond my normal limits made me feel alive. And continuing to feel so good was helping me pump out so much writing.

The next week, the film crew came to Chase's condo. Well, I guess according to the show, it was my condo too. They didn't need that much footage because I was only going to be in a tiny part of the pilot they were pitching, but in order to get enough footage to choose from they would be there all day.

To start, the cameras were rolling on me sitting on the couch writing when Chase walked in the door with a rather large box. Following my lines I asked, "What's in the box?"

Chase replied, "A sex swing."

I enthusiastically stood up and said, "For real? I've been wanting a sex swing! Where are we going to put it?"

"I think we should put it in the guest room or the office?"

"I'm not sure it should be in the guest room where my parents stay when they are visiting."

"We can take it down for certain visitors."

Chase and I proceeded into the guest room and I pointed out a place for it to go. We pulled the sex swing out of the box and Chase started to put it together, but I had the instruction manual in my hand and told him he was doing it wrong. He was insistent that he had it under control, though. When he was ready to hook it to the ceiling we realized we didn't have a ladder so we pulled the ottoman in the guest room and put a chair on it so he could reach the ceiling. I stood holding the chair while he wobbled and put the hook in the ceiling.

Once he placed the swing on the hook he told me to get on it, but I refused knowing he had put the swing together wrong. He sat in it and I was right because his ass fell splat onto the ground. We put the swing back together following the directions this time and then hung it back on the hook. I was ready to hop on. I sat in it and the feeling of being in it turned me on. I pulled Chase close to me and whispered, "My panties are wet. I want to use this sex swing now."

Chase excused the film crew and shut the door behind them after they left. I threw off my shirt and pulled down my pants before getting back on the swing. Once I was on the swing, Chase penetrated me and swung me back and forth on his cock. I felt so free swinging around in the air like that while getting fucked. He swung me faster and faster and penetrated me deeper and deeper. I could feel him hitting spots in ways he never could before. I loved this swing and I moaned out loud in pleasure. I'm sure the film crew could hear me, but I didn't care.

After I orgasmed, Chase pulled out and came on my stomach. He looked at me and said, "You are so fucking beautiful, I just love you to pieces!"

I smiled back at him and said, "You and your cock make me so happy."

Chase said, "I hope so, baby," followed by a look of shock and a loud, "Holy shit!"

I wondered what had shocked him so much so I asked, "What?"

He said, "Look at the ground."

I scooted to get off the sex swing and when I looked down I saw my cum splattered on the ground below me. I thought I could feel it coming out of my pussy and dripping down my ass, but I had no idea there was so much. Chase threw on his clothes and walked out to the bathroom to get a towel to clean his cum off my stomach and my cum off the floor.

We took a little break and then I changed outfits; it was time to play out how to deal with a girl during her period. I didn't actually have my period, but Chase thought it would be good for guys to see how a man should treat his woman when she is on the rag. I put some tampons out on the counter in our bathroom and lay in bed with a heating pad. I acted as menstrual as I could once the cameras were rolling. The cameras first followed Chase into the bathroom where he noticed the tampons on the counter. He walked into the bedroom and said to me, "I know you have your period, but it would mean a lot to me if you did not leave your tampons all over the bathroom."

As dramatically and emotionally as I could say it, I said, "You try having a period!"

He came over to comfort me by crawling into bed with me. He said, "I'm sorry, baby, I didn't mean to upset you. I'm just not used to girl products being everywhere. How about I give you a back massage?"

The cameras turned off for a minute while I took off my shirt, but they began rolling again once my boobs were flat on the bed and nothing could be seen. Chase massaged my back for a few minutes telling me how beautiful I was and then the camera guy said they had enough footage of that scene. I wished they needed more footage. I was enjoying the back massage.

The last of filming would take place while we discussed an article I planned to write about keeping sex fresh in a relationship. We ordered in some Thai food, drank some wine, and completely acted natural, sharing ideas. It was the only point when filming that I didn't realize the cameras were rolling. It felt very natural to be bouncing ideas back and forth with Chase because we did it all the time. After the film crew got what they needed from us talking, they said it was a wrap. The filming process ended up being easier than I thought it would be.

Chase and the crew watched clips of what we had filmed to make sure they had what they needed. I didn't like watching myself on camera so I sat on the couch drinking wine and browsing Facebook while they went through the clips. After they confirmed that they had what they needed, the film crew left and Chase came over and sat next to me. He asked, "Did you enjoy filming?"

I said, "It was actually easier than I thought it would be."

Chase asked, "Did you enjoy seeing yourself in the clips?"

"I don't like watching myself on film. That's why I came over and sat on the couch."

Chase opened up his computer and played a clip of us assembling the sex swing. While it was playing he said, "Take a look at your body in this clip."

I watched the clip and thought my

mannerisms were a little awkward, but I looked good. I said, "I'm sorry I can be awkward sometimes."

"No, don't worry about your mannerisms. Look at your body."

Chase played the clip again and I looked at my body. I thought my body looked good so I was confused as to what he was getting at with making me watch the clip over and over. I asked, "What am I supposed to be looking at?"

Chase replied, "You know I think you are beautiful, right?"

I smiled and said, "Yes," before giving him a kiss.

"You are so beautiful, but do you think your body is in the best shape it can be in?"

"I like my body. Umm ... I guess I could have more muscle tone."

"Just think about that. You should always be the best that you can possibly be. I think that working out would be good for you."

"But, I never work out. Do you think I need to lose weight? I'm 5'6" and 110 pounds, I'm not sure I should lose any weight."

"I'm simply asking you to ask yourself if you are in the best shape that you can be in."

While Chase's representation was out pitching the new idea of his reality show to any and everyone who would listen, I was pounding out chapters in my book series like crazy. I was on a roll with my writing and feeling confident in it. The first book in my series had gone through several levels of editing with my new publisher and it was ready for print. I got a proof copy in the mail and the cover design looked even better than the jpeg image I had seen of it the week before. It felt so good to have my book in my hands, all finished. After calling my parents to tell them the first book in my series was finished, I sat down to read it until Chase got home. When he walked in the door, I ran to him in excitement holding out my book. He smiled at me with a look telling me he was proud. I explained to Chase that my parents wanted to come down to the city that night to take us to dinner and celebrate finishing my book. Chase said, "Let's have them come here for dinner and I'll cook."

I asked, "Don't you want to relax and let them buy us dinner?"

Chase said with sincerity, "Have them come here. I think it will be more comfortable for them when we tell them you are moving in with me."

I know we had talked about me moving in

with him with the possibility of a reality show, but I didn't realize we had made a final decision. I said, "I thought we were going to make a decision about me moving in once your show got picked up?"

"We don't need to wait for that. Aren't you ready to move in now? It seems like a waste for you to keep paying rent."

With hesitation I said, "Yeah, well, umm … it's just that moving in together seems so fast."

"Who cares? Live in the now. I always do what makes most sense for me today. You never know what tomorrow will bring."

"That's just it, what if things are different for us tomorrow?"

"Then we will deal with it tomorrow."

As much as I agreed with living in the now, I was uneasy about all of this. It was easy for him because he didn't have to pick up and move somewhere new. He just needed to make a little more space in his closet for me. I said, "It's just not that simple."

"Sure it is. You love me, I love you, and we make each other happy."

"Yeah, but what about logistics?"

"Logistics are just logistics. What do you need? I'll get you a moving company or whatever you need."

I asked, "Can we take a little step back on this for now?"

"Sure, take a little time. Call your parents and tell them to come here for dinner tonight, though. After you talk to them let's go on a date to the grocery store and get something to cook that they would like."

I gave Chase a kiss and said, "Remember

our first date started at the grocery store?"

He smiled at me and said, "It was our second date, baby."

"Oh yeah."

"My God, you are beautiful. Can I fuck you real quick before we go on our date to the grocery store?"

Chase lifted me up and I wrapped my legs around his waist while he carried me into the bedroom. Before he put me down on the bed, he kissed me passionately and then said, "I am so lucky that I get to fuck you all the time."

I replied, "I think I'm the lucky one."

Once I was on the bed, Chase pulled off my shirt and then down my pants. Before undressing himself, he looked at me like he had never seen something so beautiful and reminded me again just how beautiful I was. He always made me feel so confident in myself. I watched him undress and slowly crawl on top of me. He put his hand down on my pussy and said, "You are always such a good girl getting wet for me."

How could my pussy not be dripping wet when I had such a sexy man to look at, that made me feel so good? Chase penetrated my pussy slowly and I moaned in pleasure. The initial penetration always felt so good. He moved his cock in and out of me slowly and I could feel it growing harder by the second. He moved faster and then flipped me on my side holding my leg up by placing my foot by his neck. I looked down and watched his cock move in and out of me; going in so deep and coming out so far. Each time he pulled his cock out, I could see more and more of my cum covering it.

After several minutes of slow fucking me on the side, he flipped me over onto my stomach. I picked my hips up and he penetrated my pussy from behind. I liked when he fucked me from behind because he could hit deep spots that gave me super-intense orgasms. I relaxed, letting him maintain control of my body and taking in each moment of pleasure. Once he picked up speed, I felt my pussy tightening up, preparing for an orgasmic release. I held the tight pleasure for as long as I could, but I couldn't wait to feel the release of the orgasm. He was fucking me fast and my body was tight and ready to release, but he slowed down and told me not to orgasm yet. I said, "I don't want to wait. I'm ready!"

"Trust me, baby, don't release it yet."

I let my body relax and took my mind off orgasming as Chase continued to fuck me slowly. Once he felt that my body and pussy were relaxed, he increased speed again. Gradually, my body began to tense up in pleasure. He moved faster and faster and I almost reached the point of orgasming again when he slowed down. I said, "What the fuck? Don't stop."

"Hold back, baby."

What did he think I was? A sloth that can fuck for forty-two hours straight? I asked, "Why?"

He responded, "Just hold back your orgasm and trust me."

Chase flipped me over on my back. We were now face to face. I was a little upset because my orgasms were so much more intense when he fucked me from behind, but I was happy I got to look at his sexy body while he fucked me. He moved his cock in and out of my pussy slowly again, going deep every few thrusts. Once he picked up speed, my body began to tense up. I said, "You better not stop on me again."

He moved in and out of me deeper and faster until I reached the point where my body was so tense in pleasure that nothing could stop it from releasing in orgasmic ecstasy. When I released the orgasm, it was the most intense orgasm I had ever had. I moaned out loudly and my body seized with pleasure. I had never experienced such a release of pleasure in my life and I was so caught up in my orgasm, I felt like I had blacked out. When I came out of my orgasm blackout I said, "Holy shit."

Chase smiled and said, "How was it, baby?"

As I was still catching my breath I said, "Fucking unbelievable. I have never had an orgasm like that."

"That's because I stacked you."

I wasn't sure what he meant by stacking so I asked, "You what?"

"I stacked you. That's why I kept stopping. I built up a couple orgasms into one big one."

"Oh, so that's what you were talking about in your advanced sex life seminar."

"Yep, now that you are moving in, I can start putting more of my 'A' game on you."

If what he was giving me wasn't his "A" game, then I was in for a real treat in the future. I was unsure why he was holding out on me so I asked, "You haven't been giving me your 'A' game?"

"Not even close. That shit's my value. I can't be giving it away to any girl."

"I'm not just any girl."

"I know and that's why you will be getting more from me soon and when you and I get married, I will show you it all."

"You are going to hold out on me until we are married?"

"I can't be teaching you certain things until I know you are mine for life. I don't want other guys reaping the benefits. "

"That's a little selfish to hold out on me."

"Not at all. It's better that you learn slowly so I don't overwhelm you."

Chase got up to grab a washcloth to wipe the cum off my stomach. As he wiped my stomach, he said, "You are just so fucking sexy, I can tell you've been working out." *I laughed inside because I had not been working out.* I didn't say anything though, I just smiled. Chase then pulled me closer to him and said, "Let me fuck you again."

I pushed him away from me and said, "Get out of here. I can't feel my pussy from the orgasm you just gave me!"

"Okay, fine. Let's go on our date to the grocery store and then I'll fuck you when we get home."

Chase and I went to the grocery store and then he fucked me in the shower when we got home. He slaved away in the kitchen while I took my sweet ass time getting ready. Once I was ready, my mom texted me that they were about to pull up to Chase's building. I texted her back telling them to have the doorman valet their car, per Chase's instruction. I headed downstairs to meet my parents in front when they arrived. On our way up in the elevator my father kept saying, "What a fancy building," and when we walked into Chase's condo, my father seemed to be even more blown away. I knew the feeling. I felt awe-struck when I walked in for the first time, too.

Chase greeted us when we entered and handed my parents each a glass of wine. My father went to sit down at the counter, but stopped when my mother asked me to give them a tour of Chase's condo. I almost started to walk toward the guest room when I realized the sex swing was still hanging in the middle of the room. I whispered to Chase to go take it down while I took my parents in the other direction to show them his room. I took my sweet ass time showing off his bathroom and the view from his bedroom to make sure Chase had enough time to get the sex swing down. When my parents and I walked out of the bedroom, Chase gave me a look and a nod indicating we were all good and the sex swing was out of sight. I proceeded across the living area down the hall to show my parents the guest room and office. When we finished our tour my father said to Chase, "This is quite the place you have here."

Chase responded, "I'm glad you like it. I'm excited to have Audrey moving in soon."

Whoa. Although I was sure I would be moving in soon, I hadn't decided for sure yet. What the fuck? I told him I was going to need time to think about it. My father asked me, "Oh, how come you haven't told us?"

I responded with hesitation, "Well, Chase and I just discussed it and, well err ... I wanted to tell you tonight in person."

My mother chimed in saying, "It's a very nice place with plenty of space. I think his bedroom is the same size as your apartment, Audrey."

I'm pretty sure his bedroom is bigger than my apartment, but I love my apartment. My dad hopped back in the conversation and asked Chase, "Do you rent or own?"

"I own. I just bought it back in the end of February."

"This must've cost you a pretty penny. The dating industry must be good."

"My company is growing more and more every day."

The small talk between my father and Chase continued and my mother went and made herself comfortable in the living room. I followed her over and sat down on the couch next to her. She said, "So you two must be getting serious."

I responded, "It's been pretty fast, but there's just something about him that makes me feel alive. I've been feeling so good and writing like crazy."

She asked, "Have you finished your entire book series?"

"No, but I have something to show you." I walked over to the fireplace mantel and grabbed the first printed copy of my book. I brought it over to my mom and said, "Here's the first book in the series, printed and bound."

"Wow, the cover looks amazing. I am so proud of you, Audrey! When will it be available in stores?"

"I still have to review it and then give the go ahead to the publisher. They said it could be on shelves in as little as three weeks."

"I'm looking forward to reading it."

"Just to warn you, it is a little dirtier than my last book."

"I don't mind. I try not to think that you wrote it when I read your books. When I read your last book, your father and I fornicated three times while I was reading it."

They fornicated? Sometimes I hated how open my parents were about talking about their sex life. I guess I wouldn't write like I do if I didn't have their influence, but I still said, "Eww ... Mom, gross," and got up to see if I could help Chase with cooking in the kitchen.

The rest of the night went well and my mother left pretty tipsy after drinking at least a bottle of wine on her own. After my parents left, Chase and I cleaned up together. Chase said to me, "I just love getting to know your parents. I can see where you get your free spirit from."

"My parents are quite entertaining."

"I'm surprised you aren't as hippy-like as them."

"I have my moments."

After we finished cleaning, Chase kissed me and then pulled my dress off before picking me up and placing me on the counter. He kissed my lips again, only for a moment, before his lips slowly moved down my neck, past my breasts, and down my stomach, stopping on my pussy. I leaned back and relaxed while he used his tongue to work my clit until I orgasmed. I just loved what this man could do to my pussy.

Chase wanted to throw me a book launch party with friends to celebrate the first book in my series being published. I told him no, but he insisted. Little did I know he was going to throw me a party on a yacht. He kept most of the details of the party quiet because he wanted to surprise me. I thought Chase hated surprises, but apparently that only applied to him. While I was getting ready for the party, Chase came into the bedroom with a brand new dress, shoes and purse that he purchased for me from Bloomingdales. I was starting to get used to being spoiled by a man.

I got dressed and when I walked out of the bedroom, Chase stood up with wide eyes and told me how beautiful I looked. With butterflies running through my body I did a little twirl for him so he could see the dress he bought for me. He kissed me before reminding me just how much he loved me. We headed downstairs and a car took us to the marina. When we arrived all of my friends were already there. I walked on the boat feeling confident, but still nervous to be the center of attention. Just a few months ago I would never want to be the center of attention, but spending so much time with Chase made me see how much fun it can be.

I said hello to people as I walked onto the yacht, but I was only paying half attention to each person I talked to because I was too busy observing what Chase had put together. I'm sure his assistant, Mary, planned most of it, but the fact that Chase wanted to do this all for me made me smile. Everyone looked so nice, all dressed up. It was a rather formal affair. When I spotted my parents talking to Chase's parents, my stomach dropped a little. My parents had never met the parents of someone I was dating before. Well, no guys I dated after the age of eighteen. My mind started to run realizing just how serious Chase and I had become in such a short period of time. As much as it freaked me out, I knew I had never felt happier.

When I saw Nikki, I gave her a hug. She immediately gave me shit for not hanging out with her anymore. While she was bitching at me for disappearing into a man's world like all women do once they get into a relationship, I grabbed a glass of champagne off a tray a man was walking around with. I needed some bubbly to help keep me calm. I assured Nikki that I would start coming around more, and of course, she didn't believe me. When we walked over to say hi to Bree and Scotty Stylez, I noticed a table with about fifty copies of my book on it. I smiled at Chase and signaled him to come over by me. I asked him, "How did you get so many copies of my book?"

He responded, "I called your agent."

Confused, I asked, "You know my agent?"

"No, but I did my research and found out who she was. She wasn't going to help me get these books from your publisher, but I charmed her panties off."

"She can be a real stiff bitch, but she keeps

me in check."

"What do you think of the party?"

"Oh, Chase, it is just beautiful. Nobody has ever done anything like this for me before. I didn't realize my parents were coming, though."

"Yeah, when I told my mom about this party, she really wanted to come. I figured what better way for our parents to meet than out on a beautiful yacht, celebrating you."

It seemed a bit soon for our parents to meet, but if I really was going to move in with Chase then I needed to stop freaking out so much about tomorrow. Like Chase said, *do what feels right and makes you happy today*. Chase gave me a kiss, reminded me how beautiful I was and then walked away to go say hello to more people. I felt the boat start moving away from the dock and decided to go say hello to my parents and Chase's parents. They all welcomed me with big hugs and congratulations. Chase's mom was so excited to go home and read my book. I still couldn't believe this nice old woman enjoyed my dirty writing. She did raise a sex expert, though, so she had to be open about it.

The party went great and I was exhausted from trying to talk to everyone and thank them for coming. The boat pulled into the dock and Bree and Scotty Stylez tried to get Chase and me to go to some nightclub, but Chase said we had other plans. Once everyone was gone I asked Chase, "What are our other plans?"

He responded, "We are sleeping on the yacht tonight."

I had never slept on a yacht. I did attempt

to sleep on my father's speedboat up at the lake house when I was a kid, but it was so small and bumpy from the waves that my cousin and I threw in the white flag before midnight. I got excited for a new sexual adventure. Chase had me sit down on the deck of the boat and handed me a glass of champagne. He said, "Wait here for a few minutes."

I felt the boat begin to move away from the dock and I watched as the city moved into the distance. Chase came out from the cabin of the yacht to get me, putting his hand out to escort me. When we got down there, I saw rose petals all over the bed and battery powered candles placed sporadically throughout the room. A part of me thought how cheesy this was, but the girl part of me melted and I said, "I love it!"

Chase grabbed me and pulled me in for a long, passionate kiss. I got so lost in his kiss that I didn't even know he had unzipped my dress until I felt it suddenly drop to the floor. As we continued to kiss, I worked to unbutton his shirt. It took longer than I wanted, but it made me enjoy our lip lock even more. As I took off his belt and unbuttoned his pants, I could feel the cum slowly dripping out of my pussy. This man turned me on so much and so easily. Once he was naked, I moved down to put his quickly growing cock in my mouth, but he stopped me and said, "This is your day. I am going to take care of you."

Chase lifted me up and gently placed me on the bed. I lay back and he pulled off my moist panties. After he pulled my panties off, he could see the cum that was already exiting my pussy and said, "I love how wet you get for me."

He kissed me on the lips for a little longer before moving down to my pussy. When he got down there, I moaned with pleasure. He slowly moved his tongue up and down my labia, stopping here and there to tease my clit. I looked down at him and he smiled at me. I smiled back. I used to think being wrapped in his arms was my heaven, but at this moment I began to reconsider. His tongue just felt so good on my pussy. He knew the exact places to hit. When I felt him insert his fingers into my pussy and slowly increase the speed of his tongue, my body knew the true pleasure was about to come. I probably could've orgasmed right away, but I wanted to enjoy every movement for as long as I could. I couldn't hold back for long, though. It felt too good and my body was overwhelmed. My body tensed up and then released a slow and beautiful orgasm.

After I orgasmed, Chase gently placed a warm towel on my pussy. He pressed it firmly up against my labia as I came down from my orgasm. The heat and pressure almost preserved the orgasm and I was able to ride the wave even longer. Chase then asked me to flip over and lay on my stomach. I did as I was asked and he put some oil on my back and began massaging me. While he was massaging me, he pulled my hair aside from behind and came up and whispered in my ear, "I love you, baby."

I felt butterflies rush through my body. His breath hitting my neck and scent brought me back to our first encounter. We had come so far in such a short period of time and I couldn't believe he was all mine. While he was massaging me, I felt him slowly penetrate my pussy from behind. He moved slowly and I could feel my cum covering his cock while he moved in and out of my pussy. My body stayed relaxed and my pussy welcomed his cock in. He continued to massage me while he penetrated me, which made my body feel good all over. I again reconsidered my heaven. Maybe this was it?

After several minutes of his massaging and penetration, I felt Chase pull out. I knew he wasn't finished so wondered what he had planned next. He got off the bed and held his hand out as an invitation to come with him. I took his hand and followed his lead. We walked out to the back deck of the yacht. Chicago's skyline looked so beautiful and even though there was a little chill in the air, I knew I'd be warmed up by Chase, soon. He had me stand next to the side of the boat and spread my legs. He penetrated me, but pulled me in close to his body. He gently kissed my neck from behind while he slowly penetrated me. He said, "Isn't the view perfect?"

I mumbled, "Mmm hmm," because I wasn't paying attention to the view anymore. I was too busy concentrating on his cock moving in and out of my pussy.

Chase spun me around and then escorted me over to a cushioned chair. I lay down on my back and he crawled on top of me. He smiled at me and said, "You are so beautiful," as he penetrated my pussy. I smiled back and felt my smile get bigger the deeper he penetrated me.

He slowly moved his cock in and out of my pussy while looking at me. It didn't feel like we were fucking, it felt like we were making love. Like a scene you'd see in the movies. We gazed into each eyes with the stars shinning bright above us. No dirty talk, no spankings, and no hardcore fucking. He penetrated me slowly until he came. We connected, without saying any words and it sent shivers through my body.

My book was officially on shelves and both Chase and I were insanely busy. I was doing local readings and book signings all the while trying to finish book three in my series. On top of all that, Chase set me up with a personal trainer three days a week and they were the three most dreaded hours of my week. I had ditched out on several sessions with the personal trainer and I was starting to run out of excuses for my absences.

With both of us being so busy during the day, I tried to attend as many events as I could with him at night. Mostly though, I looked forward to going home to his house and snuggling in bed with him. I woke-up one morning and Chase was looking at me. He said he loved watching me sleep. He then pulled me over into his arms and gave me a big, morning-breath kiss. We lay talking about our busy day ahead when he asked, "Hey, when's the last time you had your period?"

I couldn't remember off the top of my head so I grabbed my phone off the nightstand and opened the Period Tracker application. I wasn't worried because I had been taking the birth control pill religiously for years. I would forget a lot of things in life, but never my birth control pill. When the Period Tracker application opened, it immediately said in big numbers that

I was eight days late. I said, "Shit, it says I am eight days late!"

Chase asked, "Really?"

I gave Chase a concerned look when I said, "Yeah."

Chase smiled, put his hand on my belly and said, "So you could have my baby in there right now?"

"Shut the fuck up. I better not!"

"We would have the cutest little baby."

"Stop it. I am going to get a pregnancy test right now."

"No, no, you stay here. I'll go. Is it weird that I hope you are pregnant?"

"Yes, stop it! I don't want to be pregnant right now!"

Chase pulled me close to him and rubbed my belly as he said, "Oh come on. We'd make great parents."

"Go get a pregnancy test now or I am going."

Chase said, "Okay," then he pulled my chin to look him in the eyes and continued, "Just remember that I love you to pieces, baby, and if you are pregnant, I am here."

I pulled away from him as I said, "Yeah, yeah, go get that test!"

Chase threw on some clothes and a hat and walked out the door. Shortly after he left, I heard his phone ringing on the counter in the kitchen. It stopped for a minute then rang again. It stopped again then started ringing again. It was his mother calling over and over and I started to worry that something might be wrong. I picked up the phone to call his mother back and make sure everything was okay when

I noticed there were several calls on his phone to and from a Kelly. I tried to think for a minute to figure out who Kelly was, but I couldn't remember meeting a client, family member, or friend named Kelly. I couldn't recall him ever talking about a Kelly. Regrettably, I decided to look at his text messages to see if there were any texts from Kelly that might refresh my memory on who she was.

As I looked at the text thread between Chase and Kelly, I noticed it went back over a week. Chase and her had been talking sexually and she had sent him a bunch of disgusting naked pictures of herself. As I read more, I noticed that they had met for a drink the night before. I began to feel sick to my stomach. I looked through the rest of his text threads and didn't see any other random women, but this was more than enough to make me ill. He was constantly telling me how beautiful I was, how much he loved me, how badly he wanted me to move in officially, and just a few minutes ago he was hoping I'd be pregnant with his baby! I didn't understand how he could act like that with me while talking to this Kelly girl in such a way.

I packed up a bag and stood by the door with my arms folded impatiently waiting for him to come home. As I stood there, I said over and over in my head, "Please don't be pregnant! Please don't be pregnant!"

When Chase walked in the door he was smiling, but after one look at me his smile disappeared and he asked, "What's wrong?"

I simply asked, "Who's Kelly?"

I saw his face turn from concerned to

scared before he asked, "Kelly who?"

"I don't know. You tell me."

"Baby, I don't know who you are talking about."

With an attitude I said, "Don't you call me 'baby' right now and don't you lie to me."

Chase asked, "Why is your bag packed?"

I ignored his question and screamed out, "Chase, who the fuck is Kelly?"

Chase grabbed my hand and brought me over to the couch. We sat down and he said, "She's nobody. She's just a girl I'm gaming."

I asked with attitude, "A girl you are gaming?"

"I have to practice what I preach and I've been out of the game for a few months so when she told me I was a scumbag I wanted to prove to myself that I could make her fall for me."

"Seriously, Chase? You are here telling me you love me, you want me to move in, and this morning that you want me to have your fucking baby and you are going out with some random girl to see if you can get her to fall for you. Are you out of your fucking mind? What if she fell for you? Then what?"

"I'd just walk away. It's no big deal. It was just some flirty texts."

"Flirty texts? You mean her sending you naked pictures of herself was flirting? How about the date you went on with her? Did you fuck her and then come home and fuck me to prove to yourself that you can fuck two girls in one night?"

"I never touched her. I promise."

"This disgusts me. I literally feel ill. I'm going home. I can't even look at you."

"What about the pregnancy test?"

I stood up totally heated, grabbed the bag with the pregnancy test in it, walked into his bathroom, locked the door behind me and opened the pregnancy test. After I sat down on the toilet, I held the cotton end of the pregnancy test in the stream of my pee and began to weep. As I uncontrollably wept, I kept saying, "Please don't be pregnant! Please don't be pregnant!"

After I finished peeing, I set the pregnancy test on the counter to wait for the results. I put my back up to the wall, slid down to the floor and cried even harder. I heard Chase knock on the door before saying, "Baby, please let me in. Let's talk about this." I ignored his plea, but he continued ... "Please let's talk about this. Let me help you understand." I heard him wiggle the doorknob. "Come on, I love you and I would never, ever do anything to hurt you."

I continued to ignore his pleas and stayed on the bathroom floor until it was time to check the pregnancy test. I said to myself one more time, "Please don't be pregnant!" And when I looked at the test, it was negative. I felt a huge sense of relief take over my body. I took a few deep breaths and tried to figure out what to do. I decided that I just couldn't look at him right now and I needed to get out and clear my head. I opened the bathroom door and he asked, "What did the pregnancy test say?"

I didn't respond. I walked past him and toward the door, grabbing my bag on my way out. He followed me vomiting out pleas for me to stay and talk to him. I said, "I can't talk to you right now. I need to go think."

While he followed me he asked with concern, "What about the pregnancy test?"

I ignored his question and shut the door behind me, but he followed me out to the elevators. He continued vomiting out more pleas for me to stay. I just stood waiting for the elevator with tears running down my face until one of the elevator doors opened. I got in and pressed "G" for ground level. As the doors shut, I just looked at him with tear-filled eyes until he was completely out of my sight. Before I got to the ground level, I wiped the tears away the best I could and walked outside to a cab. As the cab was driving away, I saw Chase come outside and run after the cab for a few moments before stopping and putting his head down.

I began to cry again and the cabbie asked me, "Is everything okay?"

I said, "I'll be okay. I just had a little argument with my boyfriend."

He responded gently, "Oh, I see," followed by asking "Music?" with more enthusiasm.

"No, that's okay."

"Where to?"

I told the cabbie my address and then stared out the window in a daze. I heard my phone ringing over and over, but ignored it because I knew it was Chase by the ringtone. When the cabbie pulled up to my apartment building, I handed him a twenty dollar bill and told him to keep the change. I walked up the stairs and into my apartment, feeling glad that I hadn't officially moved in with Chase yet. I went right to my room, dropped my bag on the floor, fell onto my bed, and began sobbing like a baby. It was one of those ugly-faced, boogerfilled, hard-to-breathe cries that I couldn't stop.

After a good half hour of getting snot all over my pillow, I took a few deep breaths and stood up. I had to get myself together because I had a book signing in a couple hours. I looked at my phone and there were twenty-seven missed calls from Chase. If my phone wasn't my lifeline, I would've thrown it out the window or flushed it down the toilet. I undressed and got in the shower. I was doing well for a few minutes, but then I began to cry again. I sat down on the shower floor pulling my knees in to cuddle myself. All of a sudden my tears turned from emotional pain to burning pain when I felt shampoo get in my eyes. It burned like crazy. I stood up to let the water rinse out the shampoo in my eyes and then I began to laugh. Only I would be dim-witted enough to let shampoo get in my eyes while I was crying. The laugh did me good and I felt a lot better.

I got ready and took a few deep breaths before leaving for my book signing at Myopic Books. Luckily, the bookstore was just a few blocks away from my apartment and it was a nice day to walk. My phone continued to ring with Chase's ringtone from my purse. I decided to put my phone on vibrate before sending him a text that simply said, "We can talk tonight." I took all the shit that happened with him that morning off my mind. I needed to be on point to interact with people and I prayed my eyes didn't look ridiculously puffy and red.

The book signing went well and I was relieved when it was over. On my way out of the bookstore, I realized I hadn't eaten anything all day. I wasn't hungry, but I knew I needed to eat. I stopped in the vegan restaurant, Native Foods, for a wrap, a carrot cupcake, and a glass of wine. I ate toward the back of the restaurant alone and the naked images that Kelly girl sent Chase just kept going through my mind. I kept visioning him on a date with her telling her she was beautiful and wonderful; things I believed he only said to me. No matter how hard I tried, I couldn't wrap my brain around why he felt the need to game this girl? Or why he didn't come to me and talk to me about feeling insecure with his game. I knew he flirted with women, he was born a natural flirt, but the innocent flirting never bothered me. This wasn't just flirting, though. This was too far.

When I left Native Foods, I decided I needed another glass of wine. I stopped at the bar that Nikki and I usually went to. When I walked in, it was empty, and I was glad it was just the bartender and me. The bartender introduced himself as Phil; he was an old man probably in his early seventies. I ordered a glass of wine and while he was pouring it he asked me, "Do you need to talk?"

I looked at him and said, "I need to punch something."

"That bad, eh? Boy problems?"

"Yep. Why are all men such sleaze balls?"

"Some men ruin it for the rest of us. What happened?"

I don't know why, but I told Phil the bartender the entire story of what happened, sparing no detail. After I finished pouring my guts out to this old man, he refilled my glass of wine and asked, "Do you love this guy?"

I said, "Yeah, that's why this hurts so bad."

"If you love him, then you need to go talk to him."

"But what do I say when I talk to him?"

"Oh, darling, I am just the bartender. I am here to let you vent. If I tell you to stay with him or if I tell you to leave him, my opinion doesn't matter. You need to do what's best for you."

"Phil, you are no help."

"I've been with my wife for forty-six years and, of course, I've looked at other women, but I've never pursued any of them. Times are changing, though, and you are involved with a dating and sex expert. We never had those in our days and we most definitely did not have picture phones."

"Sometimes I wish I lived in the good ol' days."

"You do, darling, these are your good ol' days. Now finish your glass of wine and go talk to him or spend more time crying. It's up to you."

I chugged down my wine and then asked Phil for a little more in my glass before I left. My walk home was a little wobbly, but with each step I took I felt more and more confident to call Chase. I walked into my building and when I got to my floor, I saw Chase sitting outside my door. He looked up at me, got up, and ran to me with a big hug. I was so angry with him, but I was drunk and he looked so sad with his red, teary eyes that I decided to kiss him. Chase kissed me back passionately and then I jumped up on him, wrapping my legs around him. He carried me into my apartment to my room and undressed me quickly and passionately. I lay down on my bed on my back and watched him as he undressed. His body was impeccable. He crawled on top of me and penetrated me. The initial penetration felt so good and I moaned with pleasure. He felt so good inside of me, but when I looked at his face, I realized I wasn't looking at him the same anymore. When he fucked me, it felt just as amazing as every other time, but I no longer trusted him so when I looked him in the eye it felt different. I told myself not to look him in the eye and to concentrate on his hot body instead. If this ended up being the last time we fucked, I wanted to get off. I concentrated on his shoulder, the spot on his body that turned me on more than any other spot. The curve from his shoulder to his neck was so sexy and one of the main focus points I had when we fucked. I focused hard trying to forget all that happened that day, ridding my mind of the images I saw of Kelly in his phone. Once my mind was clear and my focus was just on his body, I felt my body tense up in pleasure before releasing an orgasm. Soon after I orgasmed, I felt Chase pull out and cum all over my stomach.

After Chase came, he lay down next to me breathing heavily. I didn't look at him; I found more comfort in staring at the ceiling fan. After a couple minutes, I felt him pull me into his arms and say, "Baby, I would never intentionally do anything to hurt you and I am so sorry I did. Something like this will never happen again." I decided I should look at him and then he continued, "I honestly feel nothing for Kelly. She was all a game. I just wanted to see if the playboy was still in me."

I asked, "Did you ever once think about me when you were talking to her or on a date with her?"

Chase sounded sincere when he said, "Every single second. I thought about how lucky I was to have you, I thought about how fun it would be for us to have a threesome with her, and I thought about how I couldn't wait to get home to see you."

With an attitude I asked, "A threesome with her? Really?"

"Yeah, I thought about all those things."

"If what you wanted from her was a threesome, then you and I should have been gaming her together."

"Then let's game her together."

"Oh no, no, no. If you want to be with me, there will be no more of this sort of gaming nonsense. Why the fuck didn't you come to me and tell me you were feeling insecure with your game?"

"I don't know? I know now that I should've. I was scared."

"If what you need is to run game then you need to talk to me about it so we can figure out a way for us to both be comfortable."

"I know that now. I'm sorry. I fucked up. Please, please, please see that and let's work together."

"I feel sick over all this."

"Please don't break up with me and I promise I will show you that this was all just a terrible mistake."

"I need to sleep on it. I think you should go. I'll come over tomorrow night after I go through all this in my head."

"Can I stay here tonight and hold you?"

"I don't think that's a good idea. I need some space."

"Please, baby, let me stay. I will go crazy without you tonight."

"No, please give me my space."

"No, I'm not leaving."

"Chase, if you want this to work out, you will give me some time and space to cool off."

"I'm scared to leave. I'm scared ..." He began to cry, "I'm so scared I will never see you again."

"No matter what my decision is, I will be at your place tomorrow night. Now please go, a night away from each other will be good."

I took the night to decompress and the next day I wrote all day. I could see the hurt and anger in my words, but I let my emotions drive my story. Throughout the night and day, I received several texts from Chase reminding me just how much he loved and cared about me. I didn't respond to any of them. I wanted space for a reason and I was going to use it to write out my feelings. I'd talk to him at night when I told him I'd talk to him. What he did was so hurtful and so disgusting that he needed to feel a separation from me just a little bit to understand what I was going through.

I texted Chase that evening before I left my apartment to let him know I was on my way to his condo. I didn't want to surprise him and have him go ape shit on me again. He had been very clear that he hated surprises. I had made the decision to end our relationship. The anger was controlling my decision and I wasn't allowing my heart to have a say. On the cab ride to his condo, I gave myself a pep talk and I was feeling strong and ready to face him. When I arrived at his place, I didn't use my key to get in, instead I knocked on his door. Chase didn't answer so I knocked again, but still no answer. I began fuming inside, thinking he wasn't there, but then as I started walking back to the elevators, he opened his door. When I looked at him, he looked like complete hell, but he welcomed me in and asked if I'd like a glass of wine. I accepted the wine knowing I needed some liquid courage. I asked, "Are you okay?"

He slowly said, "I'll be okay."

I knew there was something wrong, more than him just being emotional about what had happened the day before. I walked up to him and felt his head. He felt warm, really warm, so I asked, "Do you have a fever?"

He quietly said, "I'll be okay. Let's talk."

With aggression I asked, "No, do you have a fever?"

"A slight one."

"How slight?"

"Just over 102."

"Okay, our talk can wait. Let's go lay down in your bed."

I grabbed the glass of wine he poured for me and we went and lay down on his bed. I sat up and welcomed him to lay his head on my lap. Once he lay his head on my lap, I gently ran my fingers through his hair. I realized the stress of the last two days must've triggered a fever episode and as mad as I was at him, I didn't want to see him sick and in pain. Chase looked up at me with teary eyes and said, "I love you, baby."

I responded, "I know. Did you take some pain killers?"

"Yes."

"Did you smoke your weed?"

"Yes."

"How do you feel?"

"Horrible. I can't believe I hurt you the way I did. I fucked up. I fucked up so bad."

"Yes, you did."

"Please don't abandon me. Please don't leave me. You belong to me, Audrey."

I responded, "Oh honey, how could I ever trust you again?"

"You can. I promise I will do any and everything you want."

"I wish all this never happened."

"I wish I could take it all back. You have no idea." Chase began to cry, "Please just let me make it all up to you."

As he started to cry harder, I began to feel sorry for him. With his fever, I knew that now wasn't a good time for this talk. I said, "Let's say no more and let me take care of you tonight."

He wiped a tear off his cheek as he said, "I love you so much, baby."

That night I took care of Chase, making sure he had his meds and gently rubbing his pain away. In the morning, I woke up to him watching me sleep. His fever was almost gone so I gave myself a little pep talk in my head to end this relationship and walk away, but he used his words to reel me back in. He told me how much he loved me and all the wonderful things he'd do to make up for all the hurt he caused me. I couldn't deny his sincere tear-filled eyes no matter how hard I tried. I was disappointed in myself, but I knew how happy he made me and thought that he had learned his lesson from this incident so there's no way it would ever happen again. Giving him a second chance would relieve me from ever wondering "what if?"

I had made the decision to give Chase a second chance and forgave him for his actions, but I still hadn't completely started trusting him again. I knew eventually I would, but it would be a process. The broken trust had to be rebuilt and he was working his ass off trying to rebuild it. After a few days, I still had the need to talk about our plan of action to prevent something like this from happening again. I had thought about it a lot and figured out a way that he could still run a type of game and involve me. As I was sitting at the counter watching him cook dinner I said, "Chase."

He smiled at me and said, "Yes, baby."

"I realize you have made a different career choice than most and what you do is one of the many reasons I fell in love with you. When you felt the need to go behind my back to run game on that Kelly girl, it hurt really bad. I know you think you need to run game on girls for your work, but you really crossed the line with her."

"I know and I am still so sorry."

"I have a suggestion on how you can run and practice your game with me involved."

"What's your suggestion?"

"When you hit on girls, you seduce them with only the intention to have her be a part of our threesome." Chase's eyes widened and a smile grew on his face while I continued ... "I'm

179

not ready for a threesome just yet, but I think you running your game on women with the intention to bring them into our relationship will be something we can do together."

With some enthusiasm Chase asked, "Seriously, baby, you'd be okay with this?"

"Yes, I think so, as long as we have open communication and we do it together. I mean, we are really going to have to communicate and you are going to have to promise me the moment I say something is too much, you will step back."

"I promise. God, I fucking love you. I mean, seriously, how did I get so lucky?"

As scared as I was to give him permission to go out and seduce women with the intention of trying to get them to say yes to a threesome with us, it also excited me. It gave me power over all these women because he would seduce them all the way to the point that they'd say yes and then I had the power to say that she's not the one. Furthermore, getting closer to experiencing a threesome might make it easier to write about one in the third book in my erotic romance series.

The next week at SexCon, a sex convention, I told Chase that I was ready for him to try to seduce a girl into having a threesome with us. I figured the girls at SexCon would be open sexually and easier to convince. It would be like a beginner's class for Chase. From the moment we walked into the convention, I had my eyes peeled, looking for a girl.

I went up to the stage with Chase while he waited to go on and make a quick speech. Once he went on stage, I felt myself get a little turned on watching him so confidently talk to well over a hundred people. It made me think about when I watched him speak in Las Vegas for the first time and I felt myself looking around for a place to fuck behind the stage. I noticed a little nook behind the stage and wandered closer to see if we could sneak in there to fuck. It looked like we could so when Chase got off the stage he came by me and I whispered in his ear, "There's a spot we can fuck behind the stage."

He smiled at me and said, "Give me ten minutes."

While Chase talked to the monsoon of a crowd that wanted to talk to him after he got off the stage, I went and got a drink. While I was waiting at the bar, a girl complimented my dress. I considered her for our threesome for a second, but she seemed too nice for me to let Chase game her. After the bartender handed me a fresh drink, I walked over by Chase. He was still in conversation with a group of people so I patiently waited, listening to the next speaker on stage. Once he was finished, he looked at me and grabbed my hand before we snuck around the back of the stage into the little nook. I dropped my panties and he penetrated me from behind. His cock wasn't fully erect just yet, but I felt it get harder with each thrust he made inside of me. He was quick and pulled out and came in less than three minutes. I pulled up my panties, he zipped up his pants and we walked back out like nothing had happened. I loved the thrill I got from fucking in a place we could get caught.

We walked around SexCon, stopping at booths and gathering information. Chase handed out his business card and people accepted it like candy. We got invited into the VIP area where there were go-go dancers dancing on the tables. We sat down at one of the tables and I looked at each of the go-go dancers wondering if one of them could be Chase's bait to game. They all looked too nice and I felt bad because enough men in there were objectifying them already. When the bottle service girl came over, I took notice that she was very attractive, but when she spoke to us she was a real fucking bitch. Her attitude pissed me off a little so I whispered in Chase's ear, "She's the one."

He asked, "The one what?"

I said, "Do your thing on her and try to convince her to have a threesome with us."

With a questioning look Chase asked, "Are you sure about this?"

"Do it. I feel confident, but until I actually see you do it, I won't know for sure."

Chase got up and walked over to the bottle service girl. I could tell she was giving him crap when he first approached her, but as the minutes passed her bitchy attitude slowly changed into a flirty and fun interaction with Chase. My stomach dropped and I felt ill inside. When I saw him place his hand on her hip and lean in to whisper something to her, I almost lost it. What the fuck was I doing? What was wrong with me? What girl would be okay with this shit? I couldn't do it. I couldn't be in a relationship like this. I tried to be open and let him do his thing, but this was most definitely not for me. I got up and walked toward Chase and the girl noticing she was handing him her number. I approached them, smiled at the girl to pretend like I was cool, and then grabbed Chase's hand. He welcomed me into their conversation and kissed me before introducing me by telling me her name was Samantha. I told Samantha it was nice to meet her, but then said to Chase we needed to head out. We said goodbye to Samantha and she said she hoped to hear from us soon.

After we walked out of the venue I said to Chase, "I can't do this," and tears filled my eyes.

Chase said, "Oh, baby, it's okay. I am so glad you were open to trying it, but completely understand if you aren't comfortable with it."

"I'm sorry, I really thought I'd be okay with it if I was involved."

Chase gently grabbed my face with both hands and said, "Baby, I love you so much. Don't you ever forget that. I fucked up and thought I needed to game girls, but I don't. All I want is you."

Chase held my hand tight as we walked home. He reminded me the whole way how grateful he was to have me as a girlfriend. He said we had been through a lot in the past week and both learned new things. He asked if we could just leave the mess behind us and get back to loving one another. I told him I would want nothing more.

Chase and I settled back into our pre-fight routine quickly. Chase was being extra sweet and I loved it at first, but told him he could knock it down a notch after a week. I still hadn't gotten my period so I took another pregnancy test, but it was negative. I assumed my vagina was just being nice to me this month since I had been so stressed out. Chase teased me saying he hoped the pregnancy tests were wrong and there was a baby growing in my belly.

I was home at Chase's one day, submerged in my words as I finished up the third book in my erotic romance series when I realized I hadn't showered in two days. I smelled my armpits and decided to take a break to shower. I was getting a little frustrated with what I had been writing, anyway, so a brain break would be good. I went into the bathroom and turned on the water in the shower. After I got undressed, I looked down to check out myself and I noticed the notorious nipple hair was back. What the fuck? I prayed Chase hadn't seen it, but knowing him he would've said something if he did. I dug the tweezers out of the drawer and pulled the hair out. I then checked my other nipple for any notorious hairs. I looked to be in the clear, but again wondered why I got one notorious nipple hair?

I hopped into the shower and washed my hair. Once I was finished, I lathered up my crotch with shave gel and shaved up. I did a few quick shaves on my ass crack to make sure I didn't have any notorious hairs growing between my ass cheeks. While I was slowly shaving one row at a time of my legs Chase busted into the bathroom and scared the shit out of me. I ended up putting a nice little gash in my knee. Chase screamed out, "Baby! MTV is interested in my reality show!"

I opened the shower door and popped my head out with a smile. I asked, "Really?"

Chase danced around the bathroom for a few moments like the cartoon characters Beavis and Butthead then ran into the shower with me fully clothed. He embraced my naked, wet body with a kiss as the showerhead continued its stream of water on us. I had never seen him so excited about anything. He danced some more in the shower and then threw off his wet clothes. He said, "I'm so excited. I need to fuck you. Can I fuck you right now?"

I laughed and said, "Of course," before bending over to help him get his pants off and put his cock in my mouth to make it hard. I slipped my mouth over his cock and he was still dancing around in excitement, but I kept at it until his cock was hard enough to slip in my pussy. Once it was hard, I turned around and he pushed me up against the shower wall before slipping his cock deep into my pussy. He moved in so fast that it hurt a little, but it hurt so good.

Chase danced fucked me for several minutes before my body tensed up and released in orgasm. Immediately following my orgasm, he pulled out and came on the shower floor. I turned around and kissed him. I then told him how proud I was of him for not giving up on his dream to have his own reality TV show. He smiled ear to ear and kissed me again.

We got out of the shower and we were drying off when Chase suggested we go to dinner and celebrate. I had finally showered so I was up for it. We headed out to dinner at the hip restaurant, Tavernita, and the entire time Chase carried a smile ear to ear. He kept kissing me and hugging me in excitement. I loved seeing him so happy. After dinner, he suggested we call some friends and go out to celebrate more. We both sent out a bunch of texts and headed over to Paris Club. He ordered a bottle of Grey Goose® vodka and we cheered one another to this new adventure. Slowly, Chase's friends trickled in, joining us at his table, and a little later Nikki and Bree showed up. I was very excited to see them. I always said I wouldn't be the girl that didn't have time for her friends once she got in a relationship, but I had turned into that girl.

Chase and I shared the good news with our friends and they were ecstatic about it, especially Chase's friends who also played the role of his entourage. In less than six months, I had gone from a quiet writer to girlfriend of one of the most eligible bachelors in Chicago to soon-to-be MTV reality show star. It was such a whirlwind romance, but I loved that Chase and the excitement made me feel so alive.

The next week Chase left for a meeting with MTV in New York. I decided to go back to my apartment for the couple days that he would be gone. I needed to start packing up my stuff because once my lease was up the next month I'd officially be moving in with Chase. It was so good seeing Nikki and Bree the week before at Paris Club that I decided to invite them over for a girl's night while I had some time to myself.

When Nikki and Bree came over, we sat down and talked each other's ears off. Nikki went into detail about this guy, Ron, she was dating who according to her was a "tattooed bald hunk of hotness." Bree updated us on her and Scotty Stylez' relationship and how they had recently started talking about moving in together. When it was my turn to share my secrets about Chase, I explained how exciting each and every day was with him. Nikki said, "I guess I was wrong about him and he's not a playboy."

Because of what had happened with that Kelly girl recently, I sort of hesitated when I said, "Yeah, you were wrong."

Nikki asked, "Why did you hesitate?"

I lied and said, "I didn't hesitate."

Bree chimed in and said, "Yes, you did hesitate."

Nikki dug for some gossip by saying, "Tell us. What did he do?"

I debated in my head for a few moments thinking I shouldn't tell them about Kelly because they would think badly of Chase and I liked that now they both thought he was so perfect. After debating though, I thought it might be nice to talk about the incident. I decided to tell them about the Kelly girl and how Chase was sexting her and went on a date with her. I went on to share with them every last detail of the Kelly incident, including the pregnancy scare and my attempt to allow Chase to approach women for the sake of a threesome. As I told the story, I watched as their jaws slowly dropped. Nikki looked completely appalled and Bree's eyebrows stood up high on her forehead in shock.

When I finished telling the whole story, Nikki looked at me and said, "Dude, that's fucked up."

Bree is a psychologist so she never really picks sides on anything. Normally she is very accepting of just about anything and doesn't give an opinion, but she said, "Nikki's right. That is way fucked up."

Nikki asked, "Why didn't you call or tell either of us about this?"

I responded, "I don't know. I guess I was embarrassed and worried you guys would judge Chase or me."

Nikki said, "That's twisted you got back together with him."

This talk started bringing my mind back to the emotional roller coaster I went on when it happened and I started to cry as I said, "Am I an idiot? Do you think he will do something like that again?"

Bree came over and hugged me and said, "No, you aren't an idiot. Honey, you followed your heart and that's all you can do. You believe in second chances and that's the beauty of you."

Nikki chimed in and said, "Second chances, second schmances. I think you ARE an idiot. He's gonna fuck you over again. He's a total scumbag."

I started to cry a little harder, but laughed when Bree said to Nikki, "Shut the fuck up, Nikki! If you ever really fall in love with one of the guys you are always chasing after, then you would understand that in the end love trumps all."

Nikki rolled her eyes and said, "Yeah, until it gives you herpes and you are stuck with that shit for life."

Bree asked me, "So everything is great now, though, right?"

I said, "Yeah, things have been perfect since we decided to leave it all behind us. Chase has been so great lately. He really has been and continues to try to make up for his mishap. I truly believe he is sorry and that he realized he doesn't need to seduce multiple women to show himself and others that he knows what he is talking about."

Nikki rolled her eyes again and said, "Yeah, for now. He'll get the itch again and you'll get fucked over."

Bree said, "Nikki, stop being so negative!"

I said, "I trust him. I believe he loves me and scratching whatever itch he had to scratch with that Kelly girl opened a scab and he bled from it. I think he learned from the bleeding."

Bree smiled and said, "That's why you are a writer. You always have the perfect words to describe things."

Nikki still wasn't convinced and said, "He's a picker. He'll scratch again and you will get hurt. MARK MY WORDS. You'll see."

I said, "Alright, let's move on from this conversation." I smiled real big and said, "I can't believe I might be on a MTV reality TV show!"

Bree said, "That is so awesome. Maybe you'll be the next Snooki!"

Nikki asked, "So when do you guys find out for sure if MTV is going to pick up the show?"

I responded, "Chase is meeting with them tomorrow so hopefully he will have news then."

Nikki asked, "Are you going to officially move in with him before you guys start filming?"

I said, "Yep, my lease is up next month so I am going to start moving stuff over there in the next few weeks. I'm going to miss this place. I can't believe I've been here four years, already."

Nikki said, "I feel like you already moved out months ago. I never see you anymore. We used to get together every week at that old bar and now you are all caught up in your rich boy celebrity lifestyle."

I said, "I know you miss me, Nikki, and I promise I will do a better job of making time for you guys. You know I love you more than my luggage!"

Bree said, "Aww, that's from our favorite movie, *Steel Magnolias*. We should watch that tonight."

I asked, "What, are we going to all cuddle around my iPad and watch it?"

Bree said, "I forgot you don't have a TV. You are so weird."

I said, "If I had a TV, I would never get any writing done."

Nikki said, "How are you going to watch yourself on your reality TV show if you don't have a TV?"

I said, "Chase has TV's, but I don't like watching myself on video so I probably won't watch it."

Nikki responded, "You have to watch it. What did you think of the pilot?"

I said, "I didn't watch the pilot. I watched a small clip I was in like five times before it went to editing, but that was it."

Bree asked, "Why did you watch it five times?"

I said, "Chase had me watch it and look at myself."

Nikki cut in and asked, "Was Chase trying to get you used to watching yourself on video or something?"

I said, "No, he wanted me to look at my physical appearance and then he asked me if my body was in the best shape it could be in."

Nikki asked with confusion, "Wait, what?"

I said, "I don't know, he wanted me to look at myself and then asked me if I felt good about how I looked."

Nikki asked, "What did you say?"

I said, "I just told him maybe I could tone up my muscles a bit. He got me a personal trainer to help."

Nikki said, "Audrey, he was telling you that he thinks you look fat."

I said, "No, he tells me all the time that I am beautiful and that I have the perfect body."

Nikki said, "No, he was telling you that you are fat. Bree, you are the psychologist, tell Audrey there's some psychology bullshit behind him making her look at that clip five times."

Bree said, "It does sound a little fishy.

There is a reason he had you watch that clip over and over."

I asked, "What's the reason?"

Nikki said, "He thinks you are fat."

Bree said, "Nikki, I don't think he thinks she's fat. She's 110 pounds for crying out loud. I think he's just trying to make you picture perfect for his show."

I asked, "Is that a bad thing?"

Nikki said, "Yes, of course it is a bad thing. What's he going to try to change next?"

Bree tried to change the subject back to me moving and said, "I can't believe you are moving into Trump Tower. You are so fancy schmancy now."

I wanted the subject changed so I replied, "Yeah, Trump Tower is quite an upgrade from this dump, but I am really going to miss this place."

Nikki, Bree and I continued to chat away. I was getting sick of Nikki talking smack about Chase all night so I veered the conversation away from him every chance I got. As Nikki was telling us about how she is getting laser hair removal on her ass crack, my phone rang. I knew it was Chase from the ringtone and I felt little butterflies run through my body. I hadn't heard from him since he left that morning and I was excited to hear his voice. I answered, "Hello."

Chase responded, "Hi, baby. I don't have much time to talk, but I just wanted to let you know I miss you and love you. I was just going to text you, but I wanted to hear your voice."

I smiled as I said, "I miss you too, honey."

He asked, "Are you packing tonight?"

"I started to pack, but Bree and Nikki came over and we are having a girls' night."

"Oh, that sounds fun. I met up with an old friend and we just left dinner. We are headed to some club, but I don't want to stay out late. I want to be on point for the meeting tomorrow."

I asked, "Isn't it like 1 in the morning there?"

"Yeah, these New Yorkers eat dinner late. I was starving."

"Okay, well have fun tonight. I'll call you in the morning to make sure you are up in time for your meeting."

"You are always taking care of me. I love you, and sleep tight, my beautiful princess."

"I love you, too."

I hung up the phone and Nikki's naturally nosy ass asked, "What did he say?"

I smiled as I said, "He just wanted to tell me I'm beautiful and he loves me."

Nikki said, "Barf. You guys are annoying. What is he doing tonight?"

I said, "He just finished dinner and now is going to stop in at a club with an old friend."

Nikki said, "Probably a strip club."

Bree said, "Knock it off, Nikki."

We finished a third bottle of wine before Nikki and Bree said they better head out. I walked them to the door and hugged them goodbye. They told me not to be a stranger and I promised them I wouldn't be. After they left, I packed up a few more things, feeling sad that I'd soon be moving out of an apartment I called home for so many years, but excited that I had found someone that I wanted to spend every day with. With all the men I had dated over the years, nobody came close to making me feel as alive as Chase did.

After I packed a few boxes, I ran a bath. While I was waiting for the bathtub to fill up, I sent a text to Chase telling him that I loved him. I was a bit tipsy from the wine and feeling lovey. Chase texted me back, "I love you too, baby."

I took a long relaxing bath and then pulled out my vibrator that I was sure had gathered dust since it hadn't been used in so long. I lay naked in my bed and turned the vibrator on low using it to massage my labia. I imagined Chase on top of me, slowly penetrating me, and when I increased the speed on the vibrator, I imagined him penetrating me faster and faster. I visualized his naked body on top of mine, really concentrating on how his muscles moved so sexily when he fucked me, especially around his shoulders. Once I felt my pussy get really wet, I held the vibrator with pressure on my clit until my body tensed up and pulsated with pleasure in orgasm. Before I fell asleep, I sent Chase one last text that said, "I just got off thinking about you."

He responded, "I love hearing that."

I slept soundly that night. I'm sure the wine helped, but I think I had finally become comfortable with my journey ahead. It would be an exciting one and I knew that I could get through anything with Chase by my side. Our lives tangled together quickly and we worked well together. Nikki was always doubting Chase, but after making it through the Kelly incident I had no doubts.

When Chase got home from New York, I

was dying to know how the meeting with MTV went. He told me he didn't want to tell me over the phone so I had to wait for him to get home to tell me everything. I was at his place, soon to be our place, waiting for him when he got home. When he walked in the door, I ran up to him with a big hug and kiss. I asked with a smile, "So?"

Chase smiled back and said, "I've got a show!"

I grabbed his hands and jumped up and down with him. I couldn't believe that it was finally happening for him. I asked, "When does filming start?"

"In a month or so. Let's fuck."

"Okay, okay, but I want to know everything!"

"All that matters, baby, is that I have a show. Now let me taste that pussy."

Chase kissed me passionately and as he kissed me, we made our way into the bedroom. When we got in there, we undressed ourselves quickly before he threw me down on the bed. Once I was on my back, he snuck in between my legs and started to lick my pussy. His love for my pussy made me love him even more. He quickly moved his tongue around my labia and clit and when I looked down at him, he smiled at me with such happiness. God, his tongue felt so good on my pussy. I could feel my body tensing up in pleasure, but he stopped and moved up to kiss my lips. As he was kissing me, he slowly slid his cock in my pussy and I moaned in pleasure.

He continued to fuck me, slowly, telling me over and over how much he loved me and never to forget that. When he flipped me over on my stomach and penetrated my pussy from behind, I knew I was in for a treat. He always hit the right spots so perfectly when he fucked me from behind. As he fucked me, he massaged my shoulders. It was pure heaven. He penetrated me harder and harder, faster and faster until my body tensed up. Before I was able to release in orgasmic pleasure, he stopped though and said, "Not yet baby."

I figured he was trying to stack me, but he flipped me over on my side and lifted my leg up before penetrating me again. I loved the view I had of his cock penetrating me when I was on my side. His cock looked so big next to my pussy and would disappear so deep. I watched as his cock moved in and out of my pussy, deeper and deeper, until I felt so tense inside that I begged him to let me cum. He said, "Cum for me, baby, cum all over my cock."

I let the orgasm release and take over my body. It was pure ecstasy. I noticed Chase stopped moving his cock in and out of my pussy while I came. He stayed still until I took the first breath after my orgasm before he pulled out and came all over my inner thigh. I looked at him and said, "Thank you."

He smiled at me and said, "I love nothing more than making you cum."

Chase snuggled me and reminded me how much he loved me before falling asleep with me in his arms. I stayed up for awhile and for the first time, I really appreciated his embrace. I always took his embrace for granted, but tonight after a little time away and thinking about all the drama we had been through, I truly appreciated it. Even though it was a shitty situation with the Kelly thing, after it was over, I fell more in love with him than ever before and I couldn't wait for all the new and exciting things that were coming our way.

That night, Chase was tossing and turning like never before. I held my hand up to his head checking for a fever, but he didn't feel warm. I spooned him in hopes that it would help him sleep better, but he must've had something on his mind. It was hard to sleep with his tossing and turning, but a little after 3 a.m., I finally got to sleep. I woke-up to his alarm blaring at 9 a.m. and when I opened my eyes, Chase was looking at me. He said, "You are so beautiful when you sleep."

I rubbed my eyes and said, "Thank you."

With a smile Chase said, "Let's go to Mexico this weekend."

I asked, "What?"

"I want to go to Mexico with you this weekend, just you and me."

"Okay, but why?"

"Because I love you so much."

"Alright. When are you going to tell me all the details about your meeting with the people from MTV?"

"Later. I have a breakfast meeting so I need to shower."

"Want me to shower with you? I could give you a soapy hand job."

"My cock is already getting hard, baby."

Chase and I hopped into the shower together and I gave him a soapy hand job. Once he came, he fingered me until I came. After we were both pleasured, we spent time washing each other before getting out of the shower. We dried off and as he got dressed to go to his meeting, I threw on his robe and curled up in bed with my laptop. I had woken up to such a great morning that I was feeling inspired to write. The ending of my book was on the tip of my tongue; I just needed to find the right words to end my story. Chase kissed me goodbye before he left and I immersed myself in my words.

O ver the next couple of days, I kept asking Chase for more details on how his meeting with MTV went, but he didn't offer many details. He was pretty hush on what was going to happen and seemed very distant. On Thursday night, we were scheduled to attend an event where Chase would be presented with a Divo Award from a group called Maven. I got myself all dolled up and waited for Chase to come home because we had planned to go to the event together. I was ready right on time, but Chase hadn't come home yet. I decided to pour myself a glass of wine before sending Chase a text message asking if he was running late. He responded asking, "Late for what?"

I texted back, "For the Divo event."

He replied, "I'm already at the event."

I was confused because we had planned to go to the event together. I asked, "Was I supposed to meet you there?"

He responded, "I didn't know you were coming. Can't text anymore. Need to socialize."

That was bullshit that he didn't know I was going to the event with him. We had been excited about him getting this award for weeks. I sat drinking my glass of wine for a little bit contemplating if I should put on some comfortable clothes and do some writing or if I should head over to the event by myself. Logic told me to stay home and that if Chase wanted me at the event he would've come home to get me, but my emotions and the wine I was guzzling down were telling me I should go to the event. I chugged down the rest of my second glass of wine and headed downstairs to walk to J Bar for the event.

When I walked into J Bar, I saw a few friendly faces and said my hellos, but made a quick stop at the bar for a refresher glass of wine before I went to find Chase. While I was patiently waiting for my drink, I took a look around to see if I could spot Chase. When I did spot him, I saw him closely interacting with a woman. He was smiling while whispering in her ear with his hand on her hip. My stomach felt a little uneasy watching his interaction with her. It brought me back to the moment that he and I first met and how that was how he approached me. For a moment, I felt like maybe he was just gaming me too. That maybe I was just one of his conquests?

I told my insecurities to stop talking. Yes, maybe he used his "go to" move on me when we first met, but we were dating now and he loved me. The girl he was talking to was a just a game to him, but I was real. After giving myself a little pep talk, I walked over to say hi to a fellow *RedEye* writer, Jenny. On my way, I gave Chase a little pinch on the butt to say hello. I talked to Jenny for a few minutes until Chase interrupted us and pulled me aside. He said, "You look beautiful."

I smiled and leaned in to give him a kiss, but he sort of moved to the side and offered me only his cheek. I asked, "Is everything okay?"

He looked agitated when he said, "Yeah, I'm sorry. I'm just a bit overwhelmed tonight."

I asked, "Anything I can do to make you feel better?"

"No, I am looking forward to going to Mexico tomorrow where it will just be you and me."

With excitement I said, "Me too! I am all packed."

"Good. Well, I really need to be social tonight so I'm sorry I can't be by you. Are you going to be okay on your own?"

"I can manage myself. Go do your thing."

I didn't converse with Chase the rest of the night until he came to get me to leave after the event. I don't know why, but I kept an eye on Chase all night, really noticing his interactions with other women. Before the Kelly incident, I had never felt uncomfortable with him being a flirt, nor did I ever really watch his interactions. I told myself I needed to disregard it; that I was only feeling insecure because he had been distant lately. Our trip to Mexico could only bring us closer and when we returned I'd no longer feel so distant from him.

On Friday morning, Chase and I got up early to catch our flight to Cabo San Lucas. I was ready for some sun and a few days away from writing. I had finished my book, but next was my five step editing process, which was the least fun part of writing. I knew that after a weekend away with Chase, I'd come back relaxed and ready to edit.

During the flight to Cabo San Lucas, Chase seemed agitated. I asked him if everything was okay a few times and each time he said, "Just remember how much I love you, baby."

I wasn't sure what he meant by it, but him telling me how much he loved me never got old. I brushed off the notice of his agitation, thinking it would be gone once we got to Cabo San Lucas and we were lying in the sun on the beach. When we arrived and we were settled in on the beach, Chase seemed to relax a bit. I'm sure the four margaritas we had before we actually got to the beach helped.

As we lay out on the beach, I looked over at Chase with his eyes closed, taking in the sun and the sounds of the waves, and said, "Chase, I love you."

Chase pulled his aviator sunglasses down and looked at me before saying, "Baby, I love you too and never forget that. You are my dream girl, my angel, and no matter what I will never, ever stop loving you."

His response seemed a bit morbid, but I was in Mexico, drunk on margaritas, so I closed my eyes and let myself relax into my chair. I got so relaxed that I dozed off for a bit until Pillo came by asking if we wanted another round of drinks. Of course I wanted another drink, so I ordered two for myself. After Pillo came back with our drinks Chase asked, "So how are we going to find a way to have sex on the beach?"

I said, "Let's go on a little walk and investigate."

Chase grabbed my hand and led me down the beach. We walked in silence for a little while. I began to feel like there was something Chase wasn't telling me. I asked, "What's going on in your head?"

He responded, "Don't you worry, baby, just enjoy the paradise that we are in."

"Whatever is preoccupying your mind is taking you away from me in paradise."

"I'm sorry, you are right. I came here to spend time with you and you deserve all of my attention. I'm going to put the thoughts in my head aside and just spend time with you, loving you, and appreciating you."

"Good, now let's figure out which part of this beach we are going to fuck on." We continued to walk down the beach until we spotted a small area of trees at the top of the shore. As I pointed to the area of trees I asked, "How about there?"

Chase looked up and said, "Looks perfect, but I think it will have to be at night."

"I agree, how about tonight after dinner?"

"It's a date."

That night after dinner, we stopped at the bar to take a shot of tequila and then walked down the beach. Well, we walked for a few minutes and then began to run because Chase couldn't wait to get under the trees and penetrate my pussy. We laughed as we ran and when we were under the group of trees, Chase began to take his pants off while I bent over for him to penetrate me. He said to me, "Take your panties off."

I looked around over my shoulder at him and said, "I'm not wearing any panties."

Chase smiled as he said, "God, you are so fucking hot."

Chase penetrated me deep, hard and fast. With the mix of the alcohol, fresh air, ocean waves, and stars in the sky, I came right away.

It was one of the first quickies that I was able to reach an orgasm. My pussy and body pulsated in pleasure, causing Chase to cum right after me. He said, "Fuck, your tight pussy made me cum so fast."

I looked back at him and said, "I'm sorry."

He said, "Don't you be sorry," and then he kissed me.

Chase and I walked back to the resort hand in hand and we planned to go back to our suite to take a bath together, but ended up stopping at a bar. While at the bar, we both had a few too many drinks and made friends with some Canadians. The Canadians were a ball of fun and when Chase told them about what he did for a living they thought it was great. They loved the stories he told them and I was sure that once they got home they'd be on his website paying the two hundred bucks to become members. We had our fun and then went back to our suite. The traveling, sun, and alcohol had worn us out and we were both asleep seconds after crashing down on the bed.

In the morning, I woke up and watched Chase as he slept. He was always watching me while I slept so I wanted to see what it was like. He looked so cute while he slept. I got bored after a couple minutes, though, and decided to crawl under the sheets and start sucking on his cock. When I put his cock in my mouth, I could taste myself on him from the night before, but it didn't bother me. It actually turned me on a little knowing that his cock still tasted like me. I kept sucking his cock until he woke up enough to pull me up and kiss me. We kissed passionately, not caring about our morning breath, before Chase got on top of me and penetrated my pussy. I said to him, "Fuck me hard. I want you to fuck me deep and hard until I cum."

Chase said with seriousness, "I'll fuck you hard, bitch, and I won't stop until you cum."

He did as he said and fucked me deep and hard. It felt good and I tensed up so fast that I knew I would've been able to orgasm in a matter of seconds, but I held on. I tried to embrace each thrust until I got to a point where I could no longer hold back anymore. Chase could sense that my body was ready to release in orgasm and he said, "Cum for me, baby, cum hard for me like a good girl."

I asked, "You want me to cum all over your big hard cock?"

"Cum, cum so hard that I can feel it."

I released my orgasm with a loud moan and as soon as my pussy stopped pulsating, Chase pulled out and came all over my stomach. As he was coming down from his orgasm, he looked me in the eyes and said, "Remember that no matter what, I will always love you."

I realized he had been saying he loved me and many of the times following up with words such as "no matter what." I wondered in my head if he knew something I didn't? Why was he talking to me like something was wrong? I wanted to bring it up to him, but I felt so good riding the wave of my orgasm that I decided to just let it be. We were in such a good place that I was sure I was over analyzing his words, which I had a bad habit of doing.

The next two days Chase and I enjoyed our time together. It was perfect. We were in complete and utter paradise. On the night before we left, we took a bath together and after our bath we made our way into the bedroom naked and wet before we fucked passionately. After we fucked, Chase pulled me into his arms and I welcomed his embrace. We were quiet for several minutes and I felt myself relaxing enough to the point that I was about to fall asleep. Before I completely dozed off, though, Chase said, "Baby?"

I said, "Yes, darling?"

"When we get home, we are going to have to break up and go our separate ways." I laughed thinking it was a joke, but after I laughed Chase turned me around and looked me in the eyes before saying, "I am so sorry baby." His eyes filled with tears, "I can't be with you anymore."

I said with confusion, "I don't understand."

"Just understand that I love you."

"I know you love me so why can't we be together?"

"After the Kelly incident, I started to do a lot of thinking. I am so in love with you, but in order to make my company into what I want it to be, I need to be able to be a playboy. I can't be tied down to one girl and that's why I want to do this now before we get more serious. I thought we could be together and that I could find a way to play it into my game, but my game is seducing women to get male clients so I need to be able to go out and seduce tons of women. I need to prove to myself and to the world that I am the best and that I can get any woman to want to sleep with me."

With an attitude I asked, "Are you being serious right now?"

"I am being very serious, Audrey. I love you, remember that I love you so much. But this company has to be a priority for me right now and you know that I always live in the right now. I am so fucking in love with you, but our timing is off. You were good for me yesterday, but you aren't good for me today. Maybe if we met a couple years down the road when my company would be more established things would be different, I don't know. Right now, I know I need to go out and be a playboy. I need to seduce women because that's what I need to prove to myself and that's what people who will watch my show will want to see." I began to cry. I didn't know what to say. He continued on, "My God baby, please don't cry. I wish I didn't have to do this. I don't want to hurt you. I really hoped in my heart I'd spend forever with you, but being with you isn't right for me at this time."

"Chase, this is twisted."

"I realize I can get people to love me and want to follow my show whether I am out to seduce you or to seduce hundreds of women, but it will be so much easier and fun to prove if I am seducing hundreds of women."

"The more you speak, the more you disgust me."

"Please try to understand where I am coming from."

"I hear you loud and clear. You want to ditch me so you can seduce hundreds of women to prove a point to yourself and a bunch of strangers. Get some fucking self-confidence! I'm going for a walk."

I threw on a sundress while Chase begged

me to stay and talk to him, but I was just too disgusted to listen to his words. I needed some air. I walked through the resort and on my way, I stopped at the bar for tequila on the rocks. I took my glass of tequila and walked down the beach. I walked until I reached a quiet area where I grabbed a chair and sat down. I felt sick to my stomach. Was he serious? He said he needed to seduce hundreds of women to get people to follow and love him. However, in the same sentence he told me he could be with me and get them to love him, but it was easier if he's seducing hundreds of women instead. Being with me was too much work for him? I stretched every single boundary I had for him, but being with me was too much work for him? I began to sob. It was an ugly hard cry. I had to let it out, though, I needed to release the emotion inside of me.

I lay on the chair, crying, not even knowing the emotions that were going through my head. I needed to get the emotions out so I could think clearly and make sense of Chase's words. After a good fifteen minutes of crying I took a deep breath and told myself to stop this ridiculous ugly-faced and booger-exploding cry. I made myself think of Chase's words. How he said he needed to prove to himself and others that he could seduce hundreds of women. My mind immediately went to Kelly and I began to cry again spitting out the words, "Nikki was right," over and over.

I took a few more deep breaths telling myself not to cry, but my emotions just couldn't understand. How could Chase tell me he loved me, tell me he wanted to marry me, tell me he hoped I had his baby in my belly, and then suddenly want to get rid of me? It didn't make sense to me. We worked so well together and every day he told me how much he loved me. Was our love no longer enough? Had proving a point to strangers become more important than our love?

I kept trying to clear my head because no matter what equation I came up with, I couldn't make sense of why he wanted to walk away from me. I took in the sound of the waves while I sipped on my large glass of tequila. As I was sitting on the chair focusing on my breaths and the sound of the waves I heard Chase say, "Audrey, oh baby, I've been looking everywhere for you."

I had no desire to see him so I said, "Please, just leave me alone."

Chase pleaded, "No, baby, please talk to me."

I asked, "What am I supposed to say?"

"Just tell me what you are feeling."

"I feel hurt and confused. Are you really that insecure that you need to prove to other people that you can seduce tons of women? Isn't it enough knowing that you can?"

"I thought it was, but I need to get back out in that world and show my fans proof."

"Proof? Aren't I proof enough that you can have it all? Not long ago you told me I was."

"I wish it were, but if I have this show with MTV, I can't be with you."

I broke into major tears and said, "But I've pushed every boundary I have to let you go out and do your thing. I've tried so hard."

"I know, baby, and that's what makes this

so hard." Chase approached me and grasped my hands in his before continuing ... "Please just listen to me for a moment. I know I handled the Kelly situation terribly." Hearing the name Kelly shot a pain up and down my body several times before landing in the pit of my stomach. I felt ill inside and pulled my hands out of Chase's grasp, but he continued on ... "I was so wrong by going out with her like that. When I started to feel like this relationship was hurting my game, I should have come to you first. I was completely wrong with what I did. After it happened, I got scared of losing you. Really scared and the way you forgave me was so beautiful. I love you so much that I couldn't bare the thought of losing you, but as each day passed I realized that this had nothing to do with you. It is about me and it is about what my company needs right now. I tried so hard to fight the feelings I was having inside telling me I had to let you go." Chase began to weep, but still continued ... "I fought those feelings every day, every hour for weeks. My insides are telling me that I have to do this though. I have to be single. I know you tried to find a way to let me run game while being with you, but it was just too much for you. Right now in my career I have to be out running game, I have to be seducing women."

"Seducing women is more important than me?"

"Yes, right now it is." I got up. I couldn't listen to him speak anymore so I started walking back to our room. Chase yelled out, "Wait, please, let's talk about this."

I turned back to look at him as I said,

"Chase, is this why you've been so distant since you got back from New York?"

"Yes."

"Is this why you wouldn't talk to me about your meeting with MTV?"

"Yes."

"Why would you bring me to Mexico this weekend if you were planning to leave me?"

"I brought you to Mexico so we could spend the last days of our relationship in paradise. I wanted to give you all the love I could before I let you go."

I asked, "Is there anything I can do or say to change your mind about this?"

Chase slowly shook his head back and forth as he said, "No."

"Enough said. I am going back to the room to go to sleep."

I marched away and Chase didn't follow me. Part of me was glad he didn't follow me, but another part of me wanted him to stop me. When I got to the room, I lay down on the bed and bawled my eyes out. I honestly didn't know what else to do. I felt so sick inside. How could I let myself fall for this guy so fast? I curled up into a little ball and cried until I heard Chase come into the room. I felt him crawl into bed and I used all my power to hold back my tears. As I lay in bed curled up in a ball, I felt Chase pull me in and cuddle me. I wanted so badly to elbow him in the stomach, but his embrace made me feel better. I let him cuddle me and it helped me relax to the point that I could fall asleep.

I woke up really early in the morning and Chase was still holding me in his arms tight. I lay there taking in the comfort and love I felt in his arms knowing that this might be the last time I'd feel this from him. As I lay there, I thought about all the things he said the night before and I began to weep again. As wonderful as I felt in his arms at this moment, it wasn't real anymore. I moved my body trying to break his embrace so I could get up to pack my suitcase. I couldn't wait to get home to my bed where I could be alone and cry freely.

As I worked to break Chase's embrace, he woke up and said, "Baby..."

I responded with an attitude, "Don't call me 'baby.'"

He still continued ... "Baby, just because I can't be with you right now doesn't mean I don't love you. Please understand that."

"Stop. Please stop. You pulled me into your world and made me fall in love with you."

"Audrey, you are what I wanted, but with this new reality TV show, my wants and needs have changed. Please just put your emotions aside for a minute and think about my company and career."

"I have thought about it and I think you are insecure and fucking lazy."

"Please, baby."

I said, "Stop calling me 'baby,'" before walking out the door, slamming it shut behind me. The main bar at our resort wasn't open yet, but I convinced Pedro to make me a stiff drink. I sat in the lobby staring off into space, trying to understand all of this. When I realized we needed to leave for the airport in twenty minutes, I went back up to the room to pack my suitcase. Chase was sitting on the end of the bed with our suitcases next to him when I walked in. I asked, "Did you pack my shit up?"

He responded. "Yes."

"Okay, let's go."

"Baby, please just talk to me."

"Talk to you about what? I have nothing to say. You even said last night there was nothing I could say to change your mind so why would I say a thing?"

"Just please try to understand."

"I've tried to understand and I just can't. You need to do what you need to do, Chase. Now, let's go."

The flight home was eerily quiet. I considered asking someone to change seats with me several times so I wouldn't have to sit next to Chase, but I stayed put. He tried to hold my hand during the flight, but I pulled away. He tried to talk to me, but I refused to listen. He even tried to pull me in for a kiss, but I used all my power to look away. I sat in silence just letting the tears run down my face.

When the plane began to descend I looked at Chase and said, "Is this really what you want?"

He responded, "It's what I need. I've worked to build this company for years and I have to do what's best to make the company grow."

I said, "Okay."

"Audrey, please understand. I love you so much and I don't want to hurt you."

"I keep trying to understand, but I can't. Knowing that you said you could be successful with me, but it would take more work than doing it without me makes me realize that you don't love me the way you say you do. Chasing women seems to be more important to you than me."

"It's not the chasing of women. It's making my company grow and proving to myself and others that I am as good as I say I am."

"You'd rather be desired by thousands than truly loved by one? Is that what you want for your life?"

"Audrey, look at me." Chase grabbed my chin to turn my face to look at him before continuing, "This has nothing to do with you. You are perfect and you have supported me more than anyone I have ever known. You are so amazing." I attempted to look away, but he put his hand back on my chin and kept talking ... "It truly has nothing to do with you. It's just timing, that's all."

Chase let go of my chin and I looked away. For the rest of the flight and all through customs, I couldn't look him in the eye and we didn't say a word to one another. As we were walking out of customs, more tears started running down my cheeks and I couldn't stop them no matter how hard I tried. People kept looking at me, but I didn't care. Chase and I walked outside and a black town car pulled up for Chase. He opened the door to let me in, but I refused to get in and walked away to get a cab. Chase followed me as he said, "Please let me drive you home."

I responded, "No, I can't be by you anymore."

"Please."

"No."

I continued to walk away and Chase didn't

come after me. I walked, sobbing, full of hope that he'd change his mind and come after me, but he didn't. I flagged down a cab and continued to sob the whole drive to my apartment. I heard my phone ringing with Chase's ringtone, but couldn't find the strength to answer it. I just cried and cried while the cabbie checked on me here and there in his rearview mirror. After the cab dropped me off at my apartment building, I went upstairs to my bed and cried myself to sleep. I couldn't believe what had happened and that our relationship was over. He had said so many things to me about love, marriage, and babies, but now none of that mattered.

The next morning, I woke up feeling like a semi-truck had hit me. I couldn't believe what had happened and wondered to myself if it was all just a bad dream. I got up and looked at my phone, seeing that I had twelve missed calls and six texts from Chase. I looked at the texts and they all said, "I'm sorry. Please call me, baby."

I realized that his decision to leave me wasn't a bad dream. I didn't want to call Chase back. He disgusted my mind and body. I began to cry again and in my cry I curled back up in bed. I laid there for over an hour, sobbing and trying to figure out and understand why he wanted to let me go, but I couldn't grasp it. He said he could be with me, but it would require more work. Why wasn't he willing to work for me? I wondered if things would be different if I let him pursue that Kelly girl more, but then reminded myself that I deserved a man who didn't need to seduce other women. What I needed was a man who was confident enough in himself that no matter what people said around him, he knew I was enough. A man who knew all he needed was to seduce just me. I was worthy of that kind of man.

I cried until I fell back asleep. Sleep seemed to be the only thing that helped me. It was a bad excuse for an escape from my mind, but with the state that I was in I needed an escape. I awoke to knocking on my door. I had a weird feeling it was Chase so I ignored it. The knocking continued for well over five minutes so I finally got up and opened the door. After I opened the door, I saw Chase on the other side crying. He said, "Baby, I am so sorry," before walking in and embracing me into a kiss. I accepted his kiss, thinking he had finally realized he was wrong and he didn't need multiple women, just me. As Chase kissed me, we slowly moved toward my bedroom and onto the bed. Chase undressed me and then undressed himself, all the while tears ran down both our faces. Once we were both fully naked, he penetrated me and it felt so good. He slowly moved his cock in and out of my pussy and as he did it, we both continued to cry. He kept at it, moving just a little bit faster until he came. After he came, he embraced my naked body into his arms and I accepted. As he cuddled me he said, "Oh baby, please just see how hard this is for me and how much I love you."

My heart dropped. I thought he came over because he realized he was a fucking idiot, but his words didn't indicate that. I asked, "Why did you come over?"

Chase replied, "I needed to see you."

I asked, "Why?"

"Just because I can't be with you right now doesn't mean I don't love you."

"Chase, are you trying to fuck with my head?"

"No."

"Then why are you here? Aren't you a fucking dating expert? Don't you realize how badly this fucks with my head?"

"You are right, I'm sorry. I don't want to fuck with your head."

I was disgusted that he came over to fuck me knowing that it would just mess with my head. I said, "You shouldn't be here. Please go."

Chase pleaded, "No, baby, this isn't goodbye forever, it's goodbye for now. Keep me in your heart."

I asked with an attitude, "For now? Keep you in my heart?"

"Yes, I can't leave until you understand why I have to do this."

I lied and said, "I understand. Now please leave."

He asked, "Do you really?"

I stood up and pointed to the door as I said, "Yes, now go."

Chase got up and while he was getting dressed, he said he'd have someone bring the stuff I had at his condo to me. He then said, "Thank you for understanding."

I didn't understand. In fact, him coming over and fucking me made this whole thing more confusing. If he truly loved me the way he said he did, then why couldn't he be with me? I just didn't get it. Before Chase walked out my door I asked, "Was I just a game to you?"

Chase hesitated for a second before saying, "No, well yes, at first you were." My stomach turned hearing his words, but he continued ... "Remember on our first date I told you that I wanted to conquer a woman mind, body and spirit?"

I shook my head up and down as I barely mumbled my one word answer, "Yes."

"Well, when I first met you, yes, you were a conquest. That's actually why I tried to hold out on sleeping with you for as long as I could. I really wanted to get inside of your head. I had actually planned to hold out on you longer, but I had to have sex on my birthday."

"Chase, you disgust me."

"No, Audrey, please listen to me. You may have been a conquest at first, but I fell in love with you. I truly did and I am still so in love with you."

"Then why are you leaving me?"

"I have to. I wanted us to work. I tried really hard to figure out a way to be with you and still hold the public image I need to hold. I even tried to make you a part of the reality show, but if I am going to be successful with this then you just cannot be in my life. I need to move in a different direction with my relationships. With a little time I know you will understand and embrace what is coming."

"Embrace what is coming? What is coming is getting over you hurting me."

"I didn't mean for either of us to get hurt. I really do care about you, Audrey."

"Just leave, Chase."

After Chase walked out the door he stopped and said, "Audrey, I really do care about you and I know you will never stop caring about and loving me."

I didn't say anything back. I shut the door and began crying again. I actually spent the next two days crying, eating an obscene amount of donuts, and watching ridiculously sad movies. When I was in bed in the middle of watching the movie *Terms of Endearment*, I heard my buzzer ring. I wondered who it could be and when I talked through the speaker I asked, "Who is it?"

The gentle voice in the speaker said, "Hi Audrey, its Chase's assistant, Mary. I have some boxes for you."

My body filled with pain and I began to cry. Chase sending my shit over to me made this whole thing even more real. I buzzed the front door and wiped the tears from my eyes. Soon, Mary appeared at my apartment door with two big boxes. She said, "I'm so sorry about what happened. Chase gets these ideas in his head about what he needs to do to please others. I really thought you were the one for him. Hopefully, he realizes that before it's too late. Don't tell him I said that though. I really need my job."

I said, "Thank you, Mary and don't worry I won't say anything to him," as I reached toward her to take the boxes.

Mary said, "Let me know if there's anything I can do for you."

I said, "Thank you," again.

After Mary left, I went back to my bed and cried myself to sleep. I didn't want to do anything, but sleep because I felt like everything reminded me of Chase. My heart literally hurt from the pain and my body shook with anxiety. I became a waste to the world for the next week, doing nothing but torturing myself looking at Chase's Facebook, Instagram, and Twitter pages. I watched as he checked into a place with that Kelly girl. I looked at him being tagged in photos, smiling happily with other women. I read as he tweeted one morning that a beautiful woman became cute when he watched her sleep. With each new post that I saw, I became more and more ill inside. So ill that at my darkest point my body wouldn't even allow me to breathe. I had cried so hard that my body screamed back at me and I had a panic attack. As I lay on the ground, my mind knew my body was giving out on me and my mind had to force my body to breathe. The panic attack felt like it lasted hours as my mind tried to regain control of my hurting body.

While I lay wasting away in bed one night, I heard my phone beep with a text. The certain beep let me know that it was Chase. I got up to pick up my phone and the three little words that he texted to me, "I miss you," were enough to make my heart drop to the floor. I paced my apartment up and down for a good fifteen minutes, trying to decide if I should respond to Chase's text. I missed him too; I missed him so much that my body was physically screaming at me to stop the pain, but I didn't know how to stop it. I decided to text Chase back the exact three words he had sent me, "I miss you."

Immediately after I sent the text to Chase he sent a reply saying, "I wish you were here in my arms."

I so badly wanted to be in his arms. I re-read his text a hundred times, convincing myself that he was being literal and wanted to see me. I put on some shoes, grabbed my purse, and headed out the door to his place. When I arrived at his building, I went up to his floor and knocked on his door, but there was no answer. I knocked again and Chase opened the door. He looked at me half asleep as he opened his arms to me. I shivered in emotion and he held me tight. We walked into his bedroom, lay down on his bed, and I cried in his arms. As he gently ran his fingers through my hair he said, "I'm sorry, baby," and I began to cry harder realizing that even though he missed me he hadn't changed his decision to leave me. I was such a fucking girl for taking his text literally. What the fuck was I thinking?

I realized that although Chase missed me, he wasn't going to change his mind about leaving me. I felt Chase fall asleep as he held me, but I laid there just a little bit longer cherishing the embrace of his arms and inhaling his scent. I then slowly broke myself of his embrace, kissed him on the forehead and went home. It had finally sunk in that we were over and I had to accept it. I couldn't waste another day of my life waiting for him to change his mind. I could no longer wait with hope that he'd see that he made a mistake. I couldn't spend any more of my time wishing that it wasn't over. I had to accept Chase's sudden change in want and need.

When I got home, I sat down at my computer and I began to write our story from the beginning. I wrote about how our whirlwind sex and love affair went from zero to sixty and then stopped suddenly when Chase slammed on the brake. How what Chase did for a living brought us together, but it was the same thing that pulled us apart. Barely sleeping for three days and getting my energy from donuts and wine, I wrote out each moment of our short-lived sexual love affair. I relived every last detail and with each word I wrote, I could feel my body returning back to normal. I could feel the anxiety being released.

So here I sit writing these last words with tear-filled eyes. I'm ready to move forward, but scared knowing that when I write that last word, my affair with Chase will truly become just a story of my past. I am digging deep into my soul to find more words to write just so I can hold on to that bliss he caused inside of me for a little bit longer, but I can't find any words and that's how I know it's time for my heart to let go of Chase Walker.

"Your heart just breaks, that's all. But you can't judge, or point fingers. You just have to be lucky enough to find someone who appreciates you."
                                    -Audrey Hepburn